9/15

T5-CVE-074

POLTERGEEKS

"The story gripped me from the first page and provided a dark but thrilling romp through a wonderfully constructed magical world. *Poltergeeks* is true edge-of-your-seat entertainment and I am really hoping there will be a sequel!"

*Linda Poitevin, author of the* Grigori Legacy *series*

"*Poltergeeks* rattles along at a fair old clip, shooting out thrills and spills and quite a few good jokes along the way. Sean Cummings is not just a good YA writer, but a good writer whatever genre he chooses to work in."

*Gary McMahon, author of* Pretty Little Dead Things

"*Poltergeeks* is *Ghostbusters* meets *Sabrina the Teenage Witch* with a dash of *X-Files*. A magical spell with equal parts humour, adventure and surprise"

*Sara Grant, author of* Dark Parties

"*Poltergeeks* is action and magic brewed into a fast-paced, death-defying spell of a read. Best friends Julie and Marcus make for a fantastic team with great chemistry and quick humor to balance out the dark peril in this high-stakes, do-or-die tale of witchcraft and suspense."

*Erin Kellison, author of the* Shadow *series*

"By turns funny, moving, and action-packed, *Poltergeeks* is almost too much fun!"

*Nancy Holzner, author of the* Deadtown *series*

SEAN CUMMINGS

# *Poltergeeks*

**STRANGE CHEMISTRY**

An Angry Robot imprint
and a member of the Osprey Group

Lace Market House
54-56 High Pavement
Nottingham NG1 1HW
UK

44-02 23rd Street, Suite 219,
Long Island City,
NY 11101
USA

www.strangechemistrybooks.com
Strange Chemistry #3

A Strange Chemistry paperback original 2012
1

Cover art Paul Young at Artist Partners.
Set in Sabon by THL Design.

Distributed in the United States by Random House, Inc., New York.

ISBN 978-1-908844-10-1
EBook ISBN: 978-1-908844-11-8


Printed in the United States of America

9 8 7 6 5 4 3 2 1

*For Mary-Kate,*
*you got it from the start*
*and never let go.*

Oh! but if this torturing Witch-catcher can by all or any of these meanes wring out a word or two of confession from any of these stupified, ignorant, unintelligible, poore silly creatures, (though none heare it but himselfe) he will adde and put her in feare to confesse telling her, else she shall be hanged; but if she doe, he will set her at liberty, and so put a word into her mouth, and make such a silly creature confesse she knowes not what.

*Matthew Hopkins*, THE DISCOVERY OF WITCHES

*Chapter 1*

Mrs Gilbert literally *flew* out the front door of her house. I should add that Marcus Guffman and I had absolutely nothing to do with it because frankly, I've had it with the whole irresponsible teenager thing. It's bad enough when people over forty look at you like you're planning on axe murdering their entire family just because you and your best friend since grade school are going door to door raising money for the Crescent Ridge High School Read-A-Thon.

I blame Fox News, but that's just me.

Now when I say that Mrs Gilbert flew out of the door I should probably preface everything by stating here and now that we're *not* talking about being chucked out the front door like some guy getting thrown out of a nightclub or a goon being kicked out of a hockey game. No, Mrs Gilbert was approximately six feet off the ground and actually flying in a lateral trajectory, landing squarely on an enormous bed of orange and yellow zinnias.

"What... the... hell?" Marcus choked, as we observed the screen door slam so hard the screws zinged off the hinges. Mrs Gilbert groaned as she struggled back to her feet, clearly in a daze. I rushed over to her, my backpack thumping clumsily against my back. Marcus followed close behind, clutching the aluminium clip board to his chest along with a baggie containing thirty four dollars and twenty nine cents in pledges.

"Mrs Gilbert!" I squeaked. "Are you OK?"

She brushed the dirt off the front of her pink night-gown and then adjusted the giant lime-coloured curlers in her grey hair. "Oh now, don't you worry your pretty little head, Julie Richardson," she said trying to look dignified. "I'm pretty sturdy for a senior citizen. Mind you, things like this don't normally happen to me with any kind of regularity."

I gave her a puzzled look and then glanced at Marcus who had an equally confused look on his face. "What normally doesn't happen?" I asked.

"It's probably nothing, sweetheart," she said with a cautious attempt at a reassuring smile. "My stars, are you and Marcus doing some fundraising? I'd get my purse but ... Well it's inside the house, isn't it?"

Suddenly we heard a noise that sounded like a huge jet of compressed air being forced through an equally huge hose, followed by an ear-splitting screech that raised the hair on the back of my neck. We glanced skyward just in time to see Mrs Gilbert's cat jettisoned out of the chimney at something close to Mach One, landing squarely on the highest branch of the neighbour's poplar tree.

"Slippers!" the old lady shrieked. "Lord have mercy, it's after my cat!"

"What is?" I asked, as I shielded my eyes from the morning sun to catch a glimpse of Mrs Gilbert's Siamese cat clinging to the branch for dear life.

She tightened the belt on her nightgown and glared menacingly at the front door of her house. "Now dear, it's not something that should concern you."

"It shouldn't concern us?" chimed Marcus. "Cats aren't normally launched through chimneys like they're mortar rounds."

"Marcus Robert Guffman, don't you *dare* take that tone with me young man!" she snapped. "Just because I'm a little old biddy doesn't mean I can't give you a lesson you won't soon forget!"

He gave her a sheepish look. "Sorry ma'am," he said quietly.

The old lady let out an impatient sigh and glanced back at her flower bed. "Well this just tops everything. Look at my zinnias! They're ruined! It's one thing to learn that your house is haunted on a Sunday morning, it's another thing entirely to wind up being tossed out the front door like a bag of trash!"

I did a double take as I watched the curtains on her bay window repeatedly open and close like someone was pulling on the cord to amuse themselves.

"Did you say haunted?" I asked in a suspicious voice as I slipped my backpack off my shoulders.

Mrs Gilbert gave me a single nod and pursed her lips tightly. "That's the only explanation I can find for it, Julie. It all started about half an hour ago when I went to the kitchen to make a cup of tea. The dishes started rattling and then the walls started pounding. I've never seen anything like it. I'd appreciate it if you'd perhaps keep this to yourself. I'm not fond of people thinking I'm the token crazy woman on the block."

I gave Marcus a look that told him to keep Mrs Gilbert distracted for a few moments. He nodded firmly as he stuffed the collection bag into his jeans.

"Er... Mrs Gilbert, let's go to the neighbour's yard and see if I can't get Slippers out of that tree. Julie, I'll catch up with you after."

I clenched my jaw tightly as Marcus led Mrs Gilbert up the front path and then turned my attention to the house.

As I watched the blinds in the bedroom window spinning like a turbine, I decided that whatever launched Mrs Gilbert and her cat from the modest bungalow wasn't your average run-of-the-mill ghost. In fact, I was pretty sure that a poltergeist had taken up residence in the poor woman's home and it clearly regarded little old ladies in green curlers – not to mention Siamese cats – as nothing more than a mere nuisance.

If Mrs Gilbert had any hope of getting back into her house, I had two options: try to identify the source of spiritual energy that gave the poltergeist the ability to interact with the mortal world, or I'd have to conduct an exorcism and *that* would guarantee me yet another blast from Mom if she found out. Still, it was a risk I was willing to take because *nobody*, supernatural or otherwise, puts the boots to senior citizens in my neighbourhood if I have anything to say about it. I reached into my backpack for the old copper amulet my mother had given me on my twelfth birthday and found it nestled between my textbook on the Enlightenment and a lukewarm bottle of Coca-Cola. I cleaned it off with my T-shirt and then I dropped the bag on the walk and cautiously approached the front door of the house, holding out the amulet for protection in case a TV set flew out the door and nailed me square in the head. The amulet, by the way, doesn't possess any magical qualities. It simply acts as a focus point for me to draw upon my spirit and invoke a spell or channel magical energy onto a target of opportunity.

Oh yeah, I'm a witch; a pretty good one, actually, though Mom keeps reminding me that I'm still her apprentice and that drives me nuts because it's almost like she's rubbing my face in it, you know? As for magic, well, each person alive carries a measure of supernatural energy deep inside. Some people say that it's your soul while others call it living energy, but it's really all the same. Everyone has the potential to sling magic around, but very few people learn how to harness their spirit and channel that energy into feats that basically defy everything we've been led to believe about the world around us. It's actually pretty cool when you think about it, but as with all forms of energy, its use comes with a cost. If you draw on your spirit too much you can literally burn up – burn up as in bursting into flames. Ever hear of spontaneous human combustion? Yeah – that was probably a practitioner who burned up because they drew on their spirit past the point of no return.

And I'm not that stupid.

I could feel spectral energy crackling around me like tiny jolts of electricity with each step I took closer to the door, and I wondered for half a second if what I was about to do might possibly be better suited to a more advanced practitioner.

OK, maybe more like five seconds.

Bear in mind that I wasn't entirely sure *what* I was going to do when I got to the door because I'd never dealt with a malevolent entity before. Hell, I should have probably headed home with my tail between my legs, but then I'd be forced to play second fiddle to Mom while she dealt with Mrs Gilbert's little problem. No, I was going to deal with this – whatever *this* was – on my own.

Or so I thought.

I had just placed my foot on the first concrete step when the spinning window blinds suddenly stopped and the front door opened with a loud click. An ice-cold gust of foul air blew through my hair and I narrowed my eyes as I poked my head into the doorway. My stomach churned as I felt a very large and very old supernatural presence, like decades worth of dust on an old steam trunk in an attic. I couldn't tell if it meant me any harm, but I wasn't about to take any chances. It had, after all, punted Mrs Gilbert from the house and at this moment it was probably sizing me up since I give off a magical signature that blazes like a supernova when I'm freaked right out.

Naturally, I just *had* to go inside and that's when it became abundantly clear to me that I probably should have called for backup.

Awesome.

## Chapter 2

Just because I'm a witch doesn't mean that I can't get in over my head when it comes to the supernatural. The first clue that I should have probably, God, *called for my mother*, was when I saw Mrs Gilbert's sofa hovering about two feet above the rose-coloured carpet in her living room. Of course, every stick of furniture was floating but the sofa, being the largest object, immediately drew my attention. I took a tentative step forward, and the sofa immediately spun around so that its polished oak feet were pointing at the ceiling. I held out my amulet and grated my teeth together as I increased my concentration. Somewhere inside the house was the source of the poltergeist's energy, I just needed to home in on it.

I clutched the copper amulet tightly in my right hand and drew on my spirit. I could feel the swirl of spectral energy brushing against my skin, so I shut my eyes tight and cleared my mind. Within seconds the temperature inside Mrs Gilbert's house dropped like a stone. I intensified my focus, directing my senses through the curtain of shadow that separates the spirit world from the mortal plane. In seconds I'd detected the source of supernatural energy: the kitchen.

"Well here goes nothing," I said, exhaling a shaky breath as I headed up a narrow hallway. No sooner had I reached the kitchen when Mrs Gilbert's stainless steel refrigerator slid across the chequered floor with a screech. The fridge door swung open and a jug of milk sailed past my head, smashing against a bookshelf. I dove for cover as a series of Tupperware containers flew off the counter. A dozen brown eggs splattered across the ceiling, the yolks dribbling down the powder-pink walls.

"Nobody likes a show-off!" I barked. "I'm coming into this kitchen whether you like it or not, so you might as well just stop this lame haunted-house routine right now!"

Apparently the poltergeist heard me.

I watched as a set of multicoloured alphabet fridge magnets floated through the air and rearranged themselves into two simple words that sent a chill up my spine:

*L-E-A-V-E  N-O-W*

At least the poltergeist was talking to me, which had to count for something. Rather than enter the kitchen, I decided to press the spirit for information.

"Spirit, what are you doing in the world of the living?" I asked, trying to sound like I wasn't intimidated.

The letters slowly rearranged themselves until another word formed:

*L-O-S-T*

"You're lost?" I was puzzled. "Spirits aren't supposed to become lost, so where *should* you be?"

The letters floated to within arms' reach and assembled into a pair of words that told me this was not your average poltergeist:

*A-T* and then *R-E-S-T*.

At rest? This wasn't a malevolent presence. If anything it was the spirit of some poor, departed soul that should have crossed over but either chose not to or wasn't being allowed to. I decided to ask it one more question before offering assistance. Just as I was about to open my mouth, a set of enamel bake ware flew out of a cupboard and slid across the floor.

I blinked a few times, half-hoping I wouldn't get beaned with a frying pan and said, "Spirit, were you on the other side? Did you cross over?"

The floating alphabet rearranged itself again.

*Y-E-S*

Holy shit!

I gulped as a surge of panic seized me. Someone had *meant* for this to happen. The spirit seemed to be lost and the poltergeist activity was either a cry for help to the living or a kind of supernatural rage at having been sucked back into the mortal world, I wasn't sure which.

And I had a right to feel panic, too.

While I'm still an apprentice witch, I'm old enough to know that pulling spirits who've passed on back into the world of the living requires boatloads of skill and is almost *always* done for a sinister purpose. More often than not, it's black magic – as black as it gets. I wasn't dumb enough to try to conduct an exorcism that would send the spirit back to the other side, because whoever or whatever had yanked it into the mortal realm would detect my magic, and they could easily send a counter-spell that could do something nasty like... Oh, how about kill me? If Mrs Gilbert was going to get back into her house, I had to figure out a way to get the spirit to leave without being detected by whoever sent it here.

Suddenly every single cupboard door in the kitchen swung open and then slammed shut with a deafening crash. The kitchen light flickered on and off like a strobe as the fridge magnets spelled out three words:

*H-E*

*I-S*

*C-O-M-I-N-G*

My blood ran cold. I stared hard at the alphabet letters and tried desperately not to freak out. There had to be a way to get the spirit out of the house before he or it or whatever the hell was coming detected my magic. I needed something to act as a proxy for the spirit to occupy, and yes, damn it all, I was going to have to ask for my mother's help after all. Then it dawned on me; Mrs Gilbert was a granny – there had to be children's toys in the house I could use. Something without opposable thumbs, because there was the very real possibility that whatever was coming might occupy the proxy as well. The last thing I needed was to get chased out of the old lady's house by a knife-wielding Cabbage Patch doll.

I raced down the hall and checked each bedroom until I found a toy chest. I threw off the lid and began rifling through until I found a plush teddy bear with movable arms and legs. I gave it a quick once-over and then I darted back up the hall and threw the teddy bear into the kitchen. It landed against the side of the fridge and slid onto the floor.

"Spirit!" I shouted. "I can get you back to the other side but I can't do it here. I need you to enter into that teddy bear and I can take you to someone who will help you cross over!"

I didn't have to repeat myself. An almighty crash shook the house as all the furniture fell to the floor at the same time, and I had to grab hold of the wall to keep myself from landing square on my butt. I felt a blast of spectral energy pass through my body as the spirit flew into the soft toy, and I allowed myself a satisfied smile. My idea actually seemed to be working.

Seconds later, the only movement in the house besides my thumping heart was the small bear's arms and legs. The stuffed animal turned its head toward me and *winked*!

"OK, *that* is too creepy."

I heard the front door open and then Marcus' familiar voice call out.

"Yo, Julie, everything okay in here? I've got your backpack and Mrs Gilbert is sitting in her car waiting to get back in the house."

No sooner had the words left his lips than the floor started shaking again. A jolt of force swept Marcus off his feet, smashing his body into the stippled ceiling with enough force to leave an impact crater.

"Julie!" Marcus gasped. All the colour had drained from his face and his eyes flashed with panic. "C-can't breathe!"

A gale of supernatural fury blew through the front hall, sending me tumbling into the kitchen. I struggled to get to my feet just as Mrs Gilbert's refrigerator toppled over onto its side, spilling its contents all over the linoleum.

*"Julie... h-help!"* Marcus choked. Chunks of drywall fell to the floor as I quickly got to my feet and reached for my magic. I pushed my senses through a thick film of dark energy that was pouring through the floor vents and spreading across the carpet like an oil slick. It pulsed and throbbed with an eerie green glow, forming an enormous ghostly hand that clamped Marcus' body tightly, squeezing the air from his lungs and smashing him against the ceiling like he was a rag doll.

I raised a spell, tapping into Marcus' terror and my own panic at seeing my best friend attacked. A wave of energy washed over my body as I lashed out at the vaporous hand with a blast of magic.

"*Subsisto!*" I bellowed, as I clamped my left hand around my amulet. A stream of power flew out of my closed fist like a five ton truck, screaming down the hall and shattering the vaporous hand. Tiny shards of malice dropped to the floor, where they dissolved into a harmless mist. Marcus fell from the ceiling, bouncing off Mrs Gilbert's sofa and landing face-first on the carpet.

"Marcus!" I shrieked, as I grabbed the teddy bear and raced down the hall. "Marcus, are you okay?"

He gave his head a hard shake and slowly rolled over onto his hands and knees. His t-shirt was ripped in about four different places and there was blood on it.

"Ow," he said quietly, as he presented me with my back pack. "Poltergeists hurt. A lot."

"This was way more than a poltergeist, Marcus." I chewed my lip. "There's some pretty badass dark magic at work here. The poltergeist is a spirit that was yanked from the other side and I think I must have pissed off whoever did the yanking... damn, you've got blood on your shirt. Are you hurt?"

"Just my feelings," he said without blinking. "My shirt got wrecked courtesy of Slippers the Siamese cat. So, was that an actual spell that smashed me into the ceiling?"

I nodded as I slipped my backpack over my shoulders. "Yep, and we need to get the hell out of here before whoever conjured it decides to take another shot at us. You didn't lose our pledge money did you?"

"No," he said. He tossed me the collection bag. "The only thing I lost is any affection I might have had for cats. What's up with the teddy bear?"

"Just call it a temporary shelter for a wayward spirit," I said. "We'll take it back to my house because I'm going to have to include my mother in this one."

"That bad?" he asked.

"That big," I said grimly as we walked out the door.

Perfect. I was going to have to play second fiddle after all.

Go Team Julie.

## Chapter 3

We got back to my place after a five-minute jaunt up the path from Mrs Gilbert's. My house, incidentally, isn't exactly popular with the neighbours, whose manicured lawns and professionally landscaped flowerbeds are a major-league contrast to the weed-infested goat farm my mom calls an *ecosystem*. Then again, ninety percent of the weeds crawling up the fence and across our driveway have a magical purpose as they are key ingredients for potions, so they're kind of necessary in our line of work. We trudged up the front path. Marcus reached for the doorknob, but I snatched his hand away at the last second.

"Don't assume those sentinels are down. I'd hate for you to lose an appendage," I said firmly.

He grunted. "Oh yeah. I just figured since your mother's car is in the driveway..."

I gave Marcus an understanding smile as I whispered a word of magic and disarmed the sentinels. "You've had a traumatic day, so don't sweat it," I said easily. "Just remember that protective spells don't distinguish between good and evil, okay? They're magical booby traps."

"Gotcha. Your forte is witchcraft, mine is physics and online gaming. You wanna remind me why we hang around together, again?"

"Number one, you're going to get me an A in physics," I said, giving him a slight nudge. "And number two, you're the voice of reason when I decide to go and do something risky and dangerous."

He grunted. "Ah, glad we've got that sorted out then."

Marcus isn't exactly suitable material for the cover of a romantic novel. He stands about five foot nine and has just enough of a mischievous streak programmed into his DNA that you wonder half the time whether he's a genius or a shit-stirrer. His clothes hang off his spindly body like bed sheets on a laundry line, but he has a kind face and a quirky smile that reveals itself when he's completely intrigued by stuff like math and science – my natural enemies.

He's known me since kindergarten and he's grown up realizing that I'm, well, not exactly like other girls. Marcus first learned about my being a witch back in grade four when I stupidly boasted that inanimate objects could defy gravity. He called bullshit so I levitated a pair of winter boots in my basement and my spell went haywire somehow. I'd just managed to raise the boots about a foot off the ground when one of them went rogue. It flew out of my magic circle and smacked him in the side of the head leaving a bump the size of a grapefruit.

He took it in his stride, of course. After my mother grounded me for three days, she realized that our secret was out; at least when it came to my best friend. So Marcus became a fixture in my magical life. Mom has established one basic rule when it comes to my best friend; namely, don't try to teach him witchcraft. Naturally I broke that rule about two weeks after the "flying boots of doom" incident. I decided to teach Marcus a simple feat of magic because in my eight year-old mind, it just wasn't fair that I was a witch and Marcus wasn't. All he had to do was to draw on his spirit and move a paper clip two inches across a smooth surface. So I drilled him for a week on how to tap into his spirit and the poor guy wound up concentrating so much that he gave himself a nose bleed every single time we tried the spell.

Marcus was heartbroken, but over time he's learned that witchcraft isn't just something you decide to take up one day as a hobby, it's basically imprinted in your DNA or something. First off, there are witches like me and then there are Wiccans. They're kind of like... How about the difference between a paramedic and a surgeon? Wiccans are a breakaway sect of witchcraft. Like us, they have covens, but they're more into pagan rituals and practicing ceremonial magic. A true witch is someone born into a family of witches who can trace their lineage back for hundreds of years. We are gatekeepers to the human world. We have a long history of doing battle with supernatural threats and we keep close watch over the compacts: agreements with the non-humans that dwell in the mortal world. All of this is done through formal witches covens and a centralized Grand Council that meets twice a year during the summer and winter solstice. You can leave a coven and go it alone as my mother and I have done, but you still fall under the authority of the Grand Council. If you break the rules, someone from your local coven comes knocking at your door. If your offence is serious enough, well… use your imagination.

The smell of horseradish seared my sinuses and brought a flood of tears to my eyes as soon as we walked through the front door. In the kitchen, Mom was hovering over a huge stock pot with a gas mask over her face, stirring a vile-smelling concoction with a wooden spoon. She's self-employed. If you Google "Calgary" and "Naturalists" you'll find Mom's web page, "Donna Richardson – Earth Healing – Herbology". There's a really bad picture of my mother's head photoshopped onto a cheesy sunset background that she uses for a web banner. She charges a hundred bucks an hour to concoct everything from healing balms to stress-reducing teas that her clients swear are better than anything you can buy at a Walmart Super Centre. The downside? That goat farm in our front yard can be seen from outer space and the neighbours are always complaining that our place is bringing down their property values.

I plugged my nose and waved my backpack in the air to grab her attention. "Mom, whatever you're boiling in that pot is going to melt the paint on the walls," I complained. "When you're done, I need your help with something, okay?"

She turned her head toward me. The gas mask made her look like a giant insect in an apron. "One minute," she said, her voice muffled. "This is almost done. I'll chat with you on the deck. Hello, Mr Guffman, you've got blood on your shirt."

"I had a brief battle with a traumatized cat I was trying to rescue," he said, pulling on his shirt collar.

"I hope you won," she said pointing her wooden spoon at the door. "You both might want to get out of the kitchen before you succumb to the stench, okay?"

Marcus and I padded down the hall to the enormous French doors leading to our deck, and stepped outside again. The teddy bear inside my backpack was rolling around, giving the bag a life of its own. I hoped the spirit wasn't about to lose patience. The last thing the residents of Lake Sundance needed was a poltergeist wreaking havoc inside the home of a witch, because it's a bit like a magical armoury in our basement. Mom has enough spell-making material stored downstairs to level five city blocks.

"Spirit... *God!* Just chill out okay?" I snapped. "We're going to figure this out in a minute so please stop whatever it is that you're doing in there."

It must have heard me because the flopping about

inside my backpack ceased. Marcus took a seat on our vinyl lounger, and the morning sun gave way to a wave of heat that told me it was going to be another scorcher of a Sunday.

"So, you figure it's a poltergeist, eh?" Marcus said, eyeballing the backpack. "I'd have thought malevolent spirits were more interested in haunting vintage homes."

"Why, Marcus," said my mother, as she stepped outside and onto the deck. "Whatever gave you the impression that poltergeists are exclusively malevolent?"

She'd rolled her long red hair into a thick bun that was fixed to the top of her head with bobby pins. Her eyes narrowed as she gazed down at the backpack and I could tell from the slight edge in her voice that my discovery had thrown a wrench into her plans for the day.

I spun around on my lawn chair and held out my bag for my mother's examination. "Sorry, Mom, we ran into this about forty minutes ago at Mrs Gilbert's house. It chucked the old biddy out the front door and launched Slippers the Siamese cat through the chimney."

Mom gave me a surprised look. "That doesn't sound like your average poltergeist," she said grimly. "Do you know the spirit's name?"

"No. Why do we need to know its name?" I asked.

She grabbed the backpack and placed it on the patio table and stepped back a couple of feet. "Because if you were thinking of conducting an exorcism, aside from being grounded for the rest of your natural born life, your exorcism wouldn't have worked."

Marcus sat up. "Why's that?" he asked. "It's a spirit. I mean, it's dead, right?"

The backpack started rolling around on top of the patio table as Mom stretched out her hands to get a feel for the spirit's spiritual signature. Naturally this rubbed me the wrong way because she was clearly laying the dramatic gestures on just a little bit too thick; possibly because Marcus was watching and definitely to remind me that she was the sensei and I was still the lowly apprentice.

"This is a minor spirit," she said, concentrating. "I don't feel any menace attached to it, so that's a good thing. The reason you need to know its name is because you can't impart your will to the exorcism spell without a name. It just won't work."

Ugh. I should have known better. Names act like a conduit for magical energies. Without knowing the name of the spirit, it would be the same thing as trying to turn on a lamp that doesn't have a bulb in it.

Mom pursed her lips tightly and studied the rolling backpack for a moment. "It seems to me we should probably glean as much information from this spirit before sending it back," she said. "I'll admit I'm kind of concerned that it manifested as a poltergeist and attacked Mrs Gilbert."

"How come?" Marcus asked. Mom had a look of genuine worry on her face.

"Because it went nuts in Mrs Gilbert's house and after I got it into the teddy bear you got drilled by some kind of dark spell," I said. "Mom is saying that it could have done any number of things, but to attack a person who is alive, well, I guess that's probably not a good sign."

Mom positively glared at me. "Marcus was *attacked*? Julie, what the hell was Marcus doing in a poltergeist infested house. He could have been killed!"

"But I didn't detect any malice, Mom," I said. I wasn't going to hear the end of this for weeks. "I even told Marcus to stay with Mrs Gilbert. This all happened just as I was about to leave!"

Marcus nodded and tried to help. "It's my fault, Mrs Richardson. I probably should have stayed outside."

Mom clenched her jaw. "Indeed. We'll talk about this later, young lady. In the meantime bring the backpack to the shed and throw it in the circle. Make sure you bind that ring good and tight because whoever pulled that spirit into the mortal world will probably be looking for it and if they attacked Marcus, they won't even think twice about attacking us."

God, I just can't win! I try to help Mrs Gilbert reclaim her house and I wind up getting chewed out in the process. Realizing that Mom was definitely going to lay into me once Marcus went home, I let out a sigh of resignation and headed to the shed with my best friend in tow.

Yep. My life rocks.

*Chapter 4*

The ring my mother was referring to is a four foot in diameter marble circle set into the floor of what she calls "the shed". It's actually a protective ring that contains or preserves whatever is inside, but it takes a whisper of magic in order for it to work, otherwise it's pretty much useless. The shed looks like your average double-wide storage barn, but that's just from the outside. If martial arts masters have a dojo to practice their craft and train a worthy apprentice, our shed is a supernatural dojo where Mom does everything from experimenting with new spells and potions to teaching me to control my magic; which tends to go a little bit nuts if I blow my concentration.

I decided it was a wise choice to call my mom in on this one, so I handed Marcus the backpack and I slipped the key into the old railway switch padlock on the shed door and disarmed the protective spells carved into the doorframe. We stepped inside and three large candles immediately lit up, giving the dusty room a warm, orange glow.

I pointed to the ring in the center of the cold cement floor. "Just put the backpack in the center of the circle, Marcus," I said.

He shuffled to the middle of the shed and gingerly placed the bag inside the ring. I knelt at the twelve o'clock position and touched the edge of the shining marble circle with my index finger with a whisper of magic. The barely audible words flowed out from my lips, charging the air with supernatural energy that tingled and hummed for a few seconds until the ring arced with a blinding white flash and then quickly snapped shut. I allowed myself a satisfied smile and I stepped back and waited for Mom to arrive.

Marcus sat down on the floor and crossed his legs. "So, uh, Julie," he said. "What happens now?"

I gave him a shrug and fixed my gaze on the backpack. "Just some low-level magic. Mom's going to release the spirit from the teddy bear and we're probably going to grill it for information."

His lips curled up into a mischievous smile. "Nice. So you're going to play good cop, bad cop, is that it?"

"More like spiritual social worker," I said flatly. "She's going to try to get its name, but more importantly, we gotta figure out whether it can offer any clues as to who yanked it into the mortal realm."

Marcus nodded and shifted his weight onto the heels of his hands. "You know, most people our age are hanging out at the mall or partying as opposed to having an intervention with a dead person."

I shrugged. "Yeah, and when they run face first into a class-five spectre that decides to crash one of their boring parties, who are they going to turn to for help?"

He raised a finger. "Good point."

The backpack continued to move as if we'd stuffed a puppy inside.

The shed door opened and Mom walked in carrying a small cast-iron pot along with a soda bottle filled with a black liquid. She knelt down beside me and placed the pot at the twelve o'clock position and then unscrewed the cap on the pop bottle. I hunched over to get a close look at what she was doing and my stomach started doing backflips the moment she began pouring the inky black liquid into the pot.

"What's that stuff?" I asked. "It smells like ass!"

"It's an extract of enchanted juniper root and sacred tallow," she said, screwing the cap back on. "If someone or something detects my magic and decides to take a shot at us while we're releasing the spirit, with any luck you'll be protected. Now smear some under your eyes. You too, Marcus."

I scrunched up my nose and gave her a disgusted look. "You're *not* serious, are you?"

She heaved a sigh as she stuck two fingers into the pot and promptly smeared some of the disgusting goop on my face. I guess that answered my question.

Marcus gingerly dipped an index finger into the pot

and applied two thick, black streaks under his eyes which made him look like an emaciated American football player.

"Yep, this stuff definitely smells like ass," he said as he scrunched up his nose. "Why around the eyes, by the way?"

Mom covered her face with the muck and said, "You've heard the eyes are the window to the soul?"

"Yeah," said Marcus.

"Where do you think the saying came from? Your soul experiences the mortal world through your eyes, Marcus. If a counter-spell somehow gets through the sentinels surrounding the shed, it could go straight through your peepers and infect the very fabric of your soul. When that happens, your spiritual essence will wind up in the hands of the person sending the dark spell, and you'll be in a world of hurt awful bloody fast. This ointment should prevent it from happening – just call it supernatural sunscreen."

I motioned for Marcus to step back from the circle as Mom wiped her hands on her apron and knelt. She was silent for a moment and then held out her hands to begin the spell. Instantly the atmosphere inside the shed tingled with energy, making the marble ring glow like a fluorescent bar. The backpack began thrashing violently within the protective circle and I reached out my left hand to feel Mom's spell take shape.

"Spirit!" my mother bellowed. "Be released and take form within my ring!"

A hazy blue cloud drifted out of the backpack and floated clumsily around the confines of the circle. With each contact, the invisible wall of magic surrounding the protective circle spat out blinding flecks of energy that bounced across the concrete floor like sparks from a welder's torch. I crawled over to the six o'clock position and watched carefully as Mom got back to her feet, her face a mask of grim determination.

And I had to admit it, she looked every inch the professional witch.

"Speak thy name, spirit!" my mother called out with calm authority. The ghostly cloud swirled around at the sound of her voice, and I could hear a faint whisper emanating from the middle of the circle. I silenced my thoughts in the hope that I could hone in on its magical signature and I couldn't quite make out whether I was hearing a male or female voice.

"John Stearne," the spirit whispered. "I was John Stearne and my time is long past. I shouldn't be here. You shouldn't be here."

Mom pursed her lips tightly and watched as the cloud of energy grew brighter, bleaching out the inside of the shed. "Why do you choose to dwell in the world of the living, spirit?" she asked, maintaining a strong measure of authority in her voice.

The cloud drifted closer to my mother, the swirling vapour crackling loudly with patterns of energy.

"'Tis not a choice," it said, this time a little bit louder. "It tore me away from my place of rest. It peels away what little remains of who I was. I sinned in life. Perhaps it is because of my sins that it demands penance from me."

"Who?" Mom asked.

"That which has always been and always shall be," the spirit said. "It tempts and it tantalizes. It does as it pleases, for that is its purpose. It fears that which is to come."

Marcus gave me a nervous look, and I motioned for him to keep calm.

"Why would someone pull a spirit into the mortal realm, Mom?" I asked.

"That's the mystery," she said without taking her eyes off the spectre. "Whoever is responsible, they're not at all concerned about flouting the natural order of life and death."

She stretched out her arms again and took a deep breath. "Spirit, are there others like you who are trapped between here and there?"

The cloud seemed to recoil as if it had been stung by her question. It reduced by half, taking it away from the magic wall around the circle, and the sparks ceased.

"I know of none," it said, this time clear as a bell. "I am missing from my place among those who went before me. The dark hand will try once more to bind me to its will. I must return to my place of rest because my time has passed. It knows where I am and it knows how to find me. You must move swiftly."

Mom nodded firmly and shifted her eyes to the middle of the spectral mass.

"Then it falls upon me to send you to your place of rest," she said, taking a deep breath. "Spirit of John Stearne, by my will I command you return to thy place of rest and blessed be!"

The spectral vapour began to swirl inside the center of the circle. It spun faster and faster, kicking up tiny dust devils until it formed a thin funnel cloud that twisted and stretched with bewildering speed. There was an arc of lightning followed by a deafening pop that I could feel in my fillings. I gave my head a quick shake and saw that all there was left of John Stearne's spirit was a small scorch mark on the floor and three or four thin tendrils of smoke drifting into the air. The shed was silent for about five seconds and that's when things became very bad, very quickly.

*"I know your name!"* blasted a disembodied voice that shook the walls. The shed door flew off its hinges and sailed through the air, breaching the protective circle. It exploded on contact, sending splinters and shards of wood across the cold cement floor. The air crackled as a series of blinding flashes sent a wave of energy out in all directions, and then everything went slow motion for a moment. I watched in horror as my mother drifted through the air, landing flat on her back. Marcus was swept off the floor, spinning end over end until he crashed into the wall. I landed in a heap and felt every ounce of air in my lungs sail out of my mouth.

It was over as quickly as it began.

"Julie," Mom called out. "Are you alright?"

I choked for air and nodded. "Yeah, Mom. You guys okay?"

She pursed her lips tightly and blinked a few times. She shifted her gaze to the debris strewn all over the floor, then slowly raised herself up to a sitting position. "John Stearne wasn't wrong about whoever it was pulled it from the hereafter," she said grimly. "And the anger in that voice, Julie – I could feel its rage. You opened a huge can of worms when you got that spirit out of Mrs Gilbert's house. This was no isolated incident."

I clutched my amulet tightly in case whatever attacked us felt like taking another swipe at the shed. "It said it knows either your name or mine. How is that possible? We're just a couple of low-profile witches. All I did was help out a little old lady."

"That's what worries me," my mother said. "Whoever it is can attack either of us without any warning at all. Dammit, how is this possible? I took every precaution!"

"I gotta get some body armour or something," Marcus groaned as he got back to his feet. "Two attacks in less than an hour, this is nuts."

I bit my lip and glanced at the circle. "It's a set-up, there's no other explanation. This was aimed at us from the very start."

Mom got up and padded over to the doorway.

"Odd that my sentinels didn't prevent the door from flying off its hinges," she muttered as she brushed her fingers across the engravings. "I can still feel a faint trace of someone's magical signature, it's strangely familiar somehow."

I cocked a wary eyebrow and looked hard at her for a moment. "Strangely familiar in what way?"

She deliberately avoided my gaze and said, "Oh, it's nothing. Just some residual magic that I can't quite put my finger on."

"Maybe the door *was* the counter-spell," said Marcus as he grabbed a broom and began sweeping up the wood splinters.

I spun around and stared at him. "What do you mean?"

"Just maybe it's possible whoever dragged that spirit into the world of the living had enough skill to turn the power of those protective spells against you. Sort of like a shaped explosive charge but with magic, you know?"

"You could be right, Marcus," said Mom. "Look at the hinges, they're bent downward, like something was pushing against them."

I ran my hand over one of the hinges and chewed my lip for a moment. Protective sentinels are designed to direct their magical energy away from a building, not into it. They're also designed to function when someone tries to breach a magical threshold; in the case of the door, someone would have to turn the doorknob for the magic to kick in. I did a quick scan of the yard and noticed that nothing looked out of place, so I held out my right hand and shut my eyes, hoping to detect the smallest ripple of foreign magical energy, but everything felt as it should. It was clear that whoever or whatever was behind the smashed door and the assault on my mother wanted that spirit badly and meant to do harm to anyone who got in its way.

"I don't know whose voice that was and I can't detect any malicious energy," I said firmly. This was something personal, Mom, what we need to do is figure out why."

She folded her arms across her chest and looked around the shed at what was left of the door. "*We* don't have to do anything, kiddo, because you have exams to study for. As for me, I'm going to be out a couple of hundred bucks to get a new door and that means we can't go shopping next weekend like we planned. Sorry, sweetheart, but Home Depot beckons."

Well that sucked.

Not only did someone use magic to attack us, now they were preventing me from hitting up the outlet mall for a new bag.

Heads were going to roll.

## Chapter 5

Someone attacked a little old lady, my best friend and my home in less than an hour – someone with an intimate knowledge of magic and enough power that they could rip the soul of a deceased human being from the hereafter and bind that soul to their will. They knew either my mother's name or mine, and I had no idea who they were or what their motive might be.

Conspiracies suck monkey butt.

Mom had been gone for less than fifteen minutes when a thought occurred to me as to how we might learn the source of the poltergeist from Mrs Gilbert's.

"What's the next move?" Marcus asked, as he began collecting broken timber from the blown-out doorway. I grabbed one of the two dozen empty cottage cheese containers Mom uses as starter pots for magical herbs and blew out any dust that lingered inside. I grabbed a small hand broom and a dustpan and then stepped into the magic circle.

"We're going to do some chemistry," I said, as I

swept up dirt and scorched teddy bear stuffing.

Marcus's face lit up like a Christmas tree. "Sweet! I'm totally down with that! Want me to run home and get my calorimeter? I've always wanted to measure the amount of heat generated by a spell – it might actually help me identify the specific elements that charge your magic. I mean, assuming there's a molecular catalyst somehow."

I carefully dumped the contents of the dustpan into the cottage cheese container. "No offence, Marcus, but this kind of chemistry would probably wreck your calobobiter thingy."

"Calorimeter," he sighed. "What are you planning to do anyway?"

"Just a hunch that tells me we might be able to trace the origin of the spirit we'd trapped in the teddy bear. With any luck, it might give us a clue about who attacked us," I said, heading out of the shed. "Follow me."

Within minutes we were downstairs in the study, a spare bedroom that doubles as a makeshift lab for anyone who deals in the business of magic.

Each of the walls has custom-built utility shelves that stretch from floor to ceiling and on each shelf there is everything from jars containing herbs or strange liquids sealed with wax paper to old Chinese food containers filled with oddly-named items like "Milk of Dill Root" or "Crow's Toe". There's a long worktable that stretches down the middle of the room and it's covered with piles of dusty spiral notebooks, beakers, flasks and, of course, candles; lots and lots of candles.

I placed the cottage cheese container on the table as Marcus sat down on a stool and gave me a disapproving look that told me precisely what he was thinking.

"You're totally setting yourself up to get a blast of shit from your mom, Julie," he warned. "If she finds out that you've decided to play supernatural detective, she'll lose it."

"We were *attacked*," I said firmly. "And did you see how Mom got all secretive back in the shed? She has a hunch what this is about and I know her, Marcus. She'll clam the heck up if I push her on it."

"Maybe there's a reason for it," he said. "I think you should back off."

I waved a hand. "I know my limitations. I'm just going to try and figure a few things out on my own, okay? That's *my* shelving unit over there with all my own spell ingredients. Do me a favour and see if you can find a small bottle labelled "distilled water". You'll also see a spool of white thread and a small box with some birthstones in it. Would you bring them over here?"

Marcus nodded and started searching through the cluttered shelving unit while I pulled my hair back into a tight ponytail. I scooped a couple of teaspoons of "poltergunk" out of the cottage cheese container and dumped it in a cold marble bowl.

"Here," said Marcus, dropping the items on the worktable. "Julie, just promise me that nothing will happen like what happened in the shed today, okay?"

"You have my word," I said, as I unscrewed the cap from the bottle of distilled water. "There won't be a problem; I'm just going to invoke a small tracking spell. Oh, one last thing… we need a map of the city. Would you be so kind as to use the computer in the den and print one off from Google Maps?"

"Alright," he said, as he headed toward the stairs. "You know, I seriously need to get a life. I'm not built for getting my butt handed to me by poltergeists or warlocks or whatever this is."

"You have a life!" I shouted. "Besides, supernatural sleuthing with me *has* to be way more interesting than chasing all the brain-dead hot chicks at school like most guys do, right?"

I pulled a small rough opal out of the box of birthstones and snapped off a length of white thread. I could hear the printer clunking away upstairs as I tied the opal to one end of the thread and laid it out beside the bowl. Moments later Marcus padded down the steps. He waved the map at me and threw me an awkward smile.

"Crescent Ridge High's population of stunning females are boring and entirely predictable," he said. "I prefer girls with above-average intelligence – that's why I hang with you. The fact that you're about a thousand kinds of beautiful is a bonus."

I snorted. "Yeah, that's me, a *Maxim* cover model waiting to happen."

There was silence for about ten seconds as I waited

for one of Marcus's trademark barbs about how bimbo reality TV stars and celebrity sex tapes aren't anything more than cheap PR stunts, but there was nothing. I shifted my gaze from the marble bowl and stared at Marcus. I continued staring for a very long moment because I honestly didn't know how to respond to his compliment. Did someone put him up to it? I narrowed my eyes as I studied his face and Marcus's thin smile immediately dissolved. He avoided my gaze, choosing instead to look down at the floor.

"Did Marla Lavik pay you to say that, because if so you can inform her I'm going to tell everyone at school that she wears granny panties!" I said sourly.

"No. Whatever... it doesn't matter," he replied, his face turning red.

Damn. He was dead serious.

I wanted to say something but I was struck dumb; partly out of the shock of anyone thinking I was actually beautiful, but mostly because I'd never known Marcus to be so candid about his feelings before. I mean, we're best friends for crying out loud! I just stood there with my mouth wide open and then I said, "Listen, Marcus, I..."

"Never mind," he interrupted. "Let's just get back to the spell."

"Good idea," I said, clearing my throat and returning to the worktable. I tried as hard as I could to put what had just happened out of my mind. The only problem was that my brain wasn't about to let that happen.

Marcus thought I was beautiful? He couldn't seriously have feelings for me, could he? I mean, he's seen me barfing all over the place when I decided it was time for me to figure out why every adult in the Western Hemisphere thinks Bailey's Irish Cream is so awesome. He even held my head over the toilet while I begged God, my mother and all known religious deities for forgiveness in between hurls. He later deleted a stupid video I'd posted on YouTube where I was drunkenly belting out the world's most terrible version of Pink's *So What* into a wooden spoon. How could he seriously think I was beautiful after *that*?

No. He couldn't have meant what he said in a romantic way. He was just being Marcus – always there, always willing to boost my spirits whenever I felt like I was the lowest form of life on the planet.

"We need to see if there is any spell residue from the stuff I collected inside the shed," I said, bringing my mind back to the task at hand. "Measure about a third of a cup of that distilled water and pour it into the bowl, will you?"

Marcus nodded and carefully poured distilled water into a beaker, and then dumped the whole thing into the bowl. I took a deep breath and drew on my magic, as I stirred the gunk from the shed into a fine grey paste.

"That should do it," I said as I took the opal and dangled it into the goop.

"What's the rock on a string for?" asked Marcus.

"This spell is called the *penndulata* – it's a very

basic locating spell that draws on the tiniest fragments of magical energy in an object. In a moment, I'm going to dangle it over the map of Calgary and wherever the goop I've slopped all over the opal drops on the map will point to places where either the former spirit has been or, if we're lucky, we might find a clue as to who pulled it from the other side."

"Will it work?"

I shrugged. "Hopefully. Maybe you might want to step back in case I blow this and we end up covered in the stuff?"

Marcus nodded as I dangled the pendulum over the map and focused on the opal. I gathered my magic and whispered, "*Seek*."

The tiny birthstone span slowly and I could feel the wispy tendrils of residual magic beginning to intermingle with the energy of my spell. A small bead of inky grey liquid rolled down the thread and dropped with pinpoint precision onto the map, followed by another and then finally a miniscule drop landed with a tiny tap. I dropped the opal back into the goop and then bent over to see where the drops had landed.

"Call me a sceptical philistine," said Marcus. "But that ain't magic, that's called gravity."

I spun the map around and pointed to the droplets for Marcus to see. "Oh there was magic at work here, Marcus," I said. "You're just unable to feel it because you don't have heightened sensitivity to magical energy."

"No, I just have near-death experiences when I hang

with you," he said sourly.

"What does the map say?"

Marcus' eyes narrowed. "The Beltline? That's where the spell came from?"

"Looks that way," I said flatly. "We're going to have to do a bit of research."

"What kind of research?"

I narrowed my eyes as I gently blew on the inky spots to dry them off. "The kind that involves figuring out if there's been any weird ass supernatural stuff going on in that neighbourhood. I need to hit some of Mom's spell books, too, because it'll help to know what kind of spell was used to yank John Stearne into the mortal world."

Marcus pursed his lips tightly as he scanned the map. "You don't know anyone that lives in the Beltline, do you?"

"Why do you ask?"

He spun the map around. "Well it just seems too convenient, you know?"

"What do you mean?"

"I mean that everything happens for a reason," he said firmly. "Don't you find it a bit disturbing that Mrs Gilbert's poltergeist dealio happened on the *same* street where we were going door-to-door and in the *same* community where a pair of witches lives?"

"You think this was aimed at me instead of Mom?" I asked in a surprised voice.

"Maybe," he said, staring at the map. "Then again,

you haven't been around long enough to make any enemies. Does your mom have anyone in her coven that might be holding a grudge or something?"

I chewed my lip for a moment. We'd been out of the covens for so long that I could barely remember the last time we took part in a gathering. I knew that from time to time we'd be visited by a "designate" – a witch whose sole purpose is to remind those outside of the covens that the Grand Council still reigned supreme under the watchful eye of the local Maven or High Priest. Mom's mood would darken whenever a designate showed up at the door and the visit would generally last fewer than ten minutes before she'd send them packing.

I shrugged. "I don't think so. I mean, the community of witches in the city is pretty small and Mom and I have sort of been keeping a low profile for years, I'd seriously doubt that anyone would target my mother with anything."

Marcus nodded. "It's still too convenient. I'm thinking maybe we expand our sleuthing and hit up Google. There's bound to be some other stuff going on in the city."

"Sounds like a plan," I said.

## Chapter 6

"You guys still here?" my mother called out.

"Yeah!" I shouted back. "Marcus and I are doing some investigatory stuff in the library!"

I could hear her padding down the steps and in seconds she was hunched over my shoulder examining the map.

"Tracking spell, huh?" she grunted. "What part of 'study for your exam' aren't you getting, Julie?"

Damn it. I hate it when she chews me out in front of people. I clenched my jaw tightly and took a deep breath because I was ready to snap at her.

"We're good for the calculus exam tomorrow, okay?" I groaned. "I just wanted to help out a bit."

"You are an *adept*," she said snatching the map from the table. "*I* decide when and if you're ready to take matters into your own hands. Damn it all, you're as bloody headstrong as your father was!"

Whoa.

Okay, clearly I'd stepped over the line because

whenever my mom invoked my late father we'd be inches away from a titanic argument that generally wound up with me stomping up to my bedroom and slamming the door. Being grounded for a week generally followed my angry outburst and then two or three days of icy silence between us.

I shrunk a little in my chair. "Yes," I said hesitantly. "It's just that the protective sentinel on the shed got blown up and what with the poltergeist at Mrs Gilbert's... I mean, whoever did this spoke to us, Mom. It knows our names!"

She cocked an eyebrow "And what's the first thing I ever taught you about what to do if someone attacks you using magic?"

"Yeah but I was just–"

*"Julie,"* she said in a tone that told me that what she was about to say was non-negotiable. "What's the first thing I ever taught you about what to do when you're attacked?"

"To never take matters into my own hands," I said sheepishly. "But it was just a small tracking spell. I wanted to figure out what we were up against."

"And you could have waited until I got home," she said sharply. "It's bad enough that Marcus was attacked at Mrs Gilbert's house. You're far too inexperienced to be going it alone. You know this."

I nodded. I glanced at Marcus and he grimaced at me. "I'm sorry," I said. "You're right and I probably should have listened to Marcus. He told me to wait."

"You got lucky this time," she said, placing a firm hand on my shoulder. "So, you figure the spell emanates from the Beltline, huh?"

"It looks that way. What do you think it means?"

Her eyes narrowed. "It means that someone or something is either holding a grudge against witches, or my sentinels malfunctioned badly. Listen, I'm going to check each protective spell I've spoken into the wards on the shed."

"Is it cool if we do a bit more sleuthing?" I asked, half-expecting her to shoot me down. "I want to do some online research and see what I can find out about any recent poltergeist activity in town."

She blinked a couple of times and waved a finger at me. "That's fine; see what you can come up with but *no* magic. Got it?"

I nodded. "Got it."

Mom headed to the backyard, so I raced up to my bedroom to grab my laptop along with a half-eaten tube of Pringles. Marcus met me in the living room and he hooked my computer into the wide screen. The laptop hummed quietly and he began searching Google for paranormal activity in the Calgary area while I thumbed through a couple of my mother's well-used spell books.

Now I'm no expert, but I do know a little bit more than the average person about poltergeists. There are two schools of thought regarding how they happen. The first one is that a poltergeist is what it appears to be; a ghostly manifestation that interacts with the world of the living. There can be a malevolent purpose behind a poltergeist's activity, but more often than not, they're just harmless spirits who are compelled to move objects around or even hide things; like your house keys, for example.

Understand that Marcus would scoff at this because it can't be proven with empirical precision, but think about it for a second. Have you ever misplaced something that you were one hundred percent certain was left where you said you left it? Maybe it's a watch or your bus pass, whatever. What I'm saying is that nine times out of ten, you eventually find that missing item and it's almost always found in a place where you'd have never thought about leaving that item in a thousand years.

I always leave my earrings in my small ceramic junk jar on top of my dresser, yet when a pair of my favourite earrings goes missing, I inevitably find one, not two, and it's usually in a dumb place like beside the toaster oven or in the pocket of a blazer that I wear only once in a blue moon. Naturally, the vast majority of us believe we stupidly misplaced the item, I get that. But when it happens to you, me, your neighbour and basically to any of the seven billion people who inhabit the planet with us, then either all of humanity is colossally absent-minded or there's a ton of supernatural activity going on that we turn a blind eye to.

The second possibility – and this is the one that Marcus likes – is that poltergeists aren't really spirits at all.

He believes that *some* poltergeist activity has a physical explanation like static electricity, electromagnetic fields or even sound waves where tremors from underground sources – say, blasting in a nearby mine – carry through the earth's crust and rattle our dishes. While I can accept that there are man-made reasons for why something that might look like a poltergeist has taken up residence in your home, he's forgetting that disembodied voices or objects floating through the air of their own accord are classic examples of poltergeist activity.

"I'm going to Google 'Beltline Poltergeist Activity' and see what comes up," said Marcus, as he clicked away at the keyboard.

In less than three seconds, the search gave us fourteen hits. The first three linked directly to YouTube, so we checked the date for each video to see which one was the most recent and we began our search there.

"Three videos isn't a lot, right?" asked Marcus.

I shrugged. "Beats me. It's possible they're all fake."

We spent the next few minutes reviewing a video that showed a roll of paper towel that was resting on top of a dishwasher flip into the air and then fall to the floor. Marcus was good enough to point out that a jolt of compressed air from off camera would have easily sent the paper towel roll tumbling and we decided it was a fake. Another video showed a closet door open a fraction of an inch and then moments later open to about a foot wide, but on closer examination we spotted the faint silhouette of a human arm inside the closet.

"Hmm," Marcus said, pointing to a link showing a blackened frame where a screenshot should have been. "What about this one? The title looks like it's written in some weird-ass form of computer programming code."

I leaned into the monitor and shook my head slowly. "That's not computer coding, it's something written using the Theban alphabet."

Marcus cocked his head and let out a grunt. "Theban, huh? What's that?"

"It's a very old and very sacred form of text used almost exclusively by witches. I need to decipher it."

He handed me a small yellow pad and a pen, and as I grabbed the other end of the pad and pulled, Marcus wouldn't let go of it. "There's just *no* freaking way this is a coincidence, Julie. We should call your mom in."

Part of me agreed with him, but I honestly didn't see any harm in translating the script or watching the video. I draped a reassuring arm over his shoulders and said, "You're probably right, but I don't think we're going to be in a world of hurt if I just translate the title. We'll decide what to do once I know what it means."

I spent the next couple of minutes scribbling down the characters from the title on my pad. I drew a line underneath and then transcribed each character with its corresponding Latin alphabet letter and then slid the pad onto the table. Marcus leaned in and read my translation aloud.

"A soul for a soul?" he said, his voice lilting up an octave. "What's that supposed to mean."

"Two things," I said, eyeballing the now translated title of the video. "Few people know what Theban writing is and fewer still would take the time to try and translate it. If you look at the number of hits the video has received it isn't exactly going viral. Click on the stats link, would you?"

Marcus emitted a disapproving grunt and then clicked on the link. A small bar graph appeared below the video and the time date stamp showed today's date.

"Someone's sending you a message, Julie," said Marcus in a wary voice.

"Because attacking us in the shed wasn't message enough. I guess there's only one way to find out what they want."

We watched closely as the video showed two golden labs sleeping soundly on a large puffy sofa.

"There doesn't seem to be much happening," said Marcus. "This looks more like it should be called 'What Dogs Do While I'm at Work'."

"Give it a second," I said. "Let's just watch."

We sat in silence for a few moments when suddenly the video went photonegative for a fraction of a second. Both dogs immediately looked up and cocked their heads to the right, as if someone was giving them commands. A half a second later, they cocked their heads to the left, their eyes focused on their unseen master.

"Oh… what a load of BS!" Marcus groaned.

We watched both dogs begin rolling left and then right on the couch with a feverish amount of energy.

As they rolled back and forth, I saw the curtains behind them flutter for a moment and then they slowly slide apart to reveal a small bluish orb hovering above the windowsill. It floated in a parallel line directly over the dogs – both still rolling around like crazy and looking like they were getting a heck of a workout. What happened next confirmed for me this video had to be the real deal.

The dogs immediately let out an ear-splitting yelp and then their tails pulled straight up like someone with a great deal of strength was tugging on them. They started wailing as their hindquarters raised up above the top of the couch and I decided this had to be unbelievably painful for both dogs since they started snapping at their tails in an attempt to get at whatever had grabbed them.

"Oh my God!" Marcus gasped. "Those poor dogs."

The worst was yet to come. In a scene that I'm certain would get the Humane Society involved, both dogs were pulled high into the air by their tails. Their howls poured through the small speakers in my laptop and I heard a low, almost guttural sounding voice that sent a knot of panic straight into the pit of my stomach.

"A soul for a soul." The voice rumbled as both dogs simultaneously dropped to the floor, landing in a stressed-out furry heap. The screen went photonegative again for a millisecond and then I saw the couch was turned upside down with the feet facing the ceiling, just like at Mrs Gilbert's.

"That's enough proof for me," I said. "Are you up to doing some more detective work?"

"Proof of what?" Marcus choked, as he minimized the browser. "You're not *seriously* thinking we should try to contact this guy, are you?"

"Why not?"

"Um… because your mom will probably lose her mind. Julie, she warned you. And then there's the whole 'you could get killed' part of it."

I threw my hands in the air. "We were targeted, Marcus! John Stearne's spirit became a poltergeist after someone yanked it into the mortal realm. Whoever was responsible attacked you with a dark spell, for crying out loud!"

"Then let someone who isn't barely in control of their abilities manage it," he said, motioning for me to calm down. "Why not tell her and get your coven involved?"

"Witches' covens suck," I said flatly. "There's a whole whack of internal politics junk we have to go through to get an officially sanctioned investigation."

Marcus blinked a few times and exhaled heavily. "You know, this is going to be unbelievably dangerous for both of us," he said warily. "What makes you think your mom is going to be okay with you doing this? I mean, Julie, that dark spell that was used to attack me back at Mrs Gilbert's house was huge!"

I nodded. "I know, but it's like you said – there's no such thing as a coincidence. I need to figure out who pulled John Stearne's spirit from the other side, and I'm thinking we should head over to the Beltline after school tomorrow and check it out."

"Whoa... wait a minute!" Marcus protested. "If you're saying there's some supernatural conspiracy involving that video and Mrs Gilbert's poltergeist, you should totally step aside."

I closed my laptop and gave Marcus a helpless look. Yes, it was true this was probably over my head, but I'd been living in a protective bubble all my life and I had no idea why. I was devoted to my craft and I worked my butt off learning how to control my magic, but every time something happened in the real world where I could make a difference, Mom would shoot me down. Maybe if I did a bit of reconnaissance, she'd learn to finally start letting go.

"I don't expect you to completely understand, Marcus. I mean, Mom's just a tad protective of me and it drives me nuts because I can take care of myself."

He nodded. "There's only one Julie Richardson in the world and your Mom is a widow; it makes sense that she worries about you."

"Yeah but I'm responsible – hell, I'm a thousand times more responsible than anyone at school. I don't do drugs or party. I stay out of trouble and I get awesome grades for crying out loud... except for calculus which I suck at."

"I know, but still. She's protective for a reason; you're all she's got."

"But I'm not a little girl anymore," I said, exhaling in frustration. "This whole thing is a chance for Mom to see that I can take care of myself. She needs to know that I can do this. Look, if there's a warlock running around town I have an obligation to gather as much information as I can so whoever it is can be dealt with. I'm not saying we're going to force a confrontation – I'm not completely nuts. But you know what? That little old lady is a victim in all this, and you are too. We'll just poke around and report our findings to my mother, okay?"

He gave me a worried look. "She's gonna flip out if she finds out that you've gotten in too deep."

"And your job is to make sure I don't drown," I said in a sugary, sweet voice. "Anyway, we're not going into combat or anything. Look, if anything even smells of danger, we'll hightail it out of there and report back to her, okay?"

"Uh-huh," Marcus groaned.

"You're safe, Marcus," I said, putting my arm around him again. "Butt-kicking witch with supernatural powers at your disposal; I've got your back."

"That's what I'm afraid of," he said.

## Chapter 7

So we fired off an anonymous email to the Beltline guy's YouTube account just to see what kind of response we'd get. We also needed a believable excuse for Mom and Marcus' parents about why we'd be late from school the next day. It was decided that we'd tell our parents about a fictitious social studies project and that we needed to take pictures of houses and apartment buildings from the Fifties. Yeah, we were being dishonest, but whatever caused the poltergeist at Mrs Gilbert's attacked both Marcus and my mom, so you'll forgive me if I take some things personally. The only way I could get Marcus to agree to participate was by promising up and down that I wouldn't engage in any witchcraft unless something took a swipe at us. Understand, of course, this wasn't because Marcus was focused on self-preservation, far from it, actually. Good ol' Marcus just didn't want me to get into any trouble with my mom.

Did I mention that he's awesome?

And of course, there was that... *whatever* it was in the basement of my house.

I'd chewed on that almost-moment at bedtime and it actually kept me awake because for the life of me, I don't always understand why Marcus sticks around. I'm the poster girl for inexplicable phenomenon. I possess a set of skills that, while not even in the same universe as someone like my mom, can still kick ass when circumstances warrant.

But what the hell *was* that? I needed some female insight, so I grabbed my cell phone and texted my girlfriend Marla Lavik. She's a Goth; very dark and terrible, but she can read people better than I can read a book. She texted me back less than thirty seconds later and told me to call her immediately, so I hit the speed dial and the phone rang just once before she picked it up.

"Hey," she said. "This better be good because it's like 11.30 at night."

"It is," I replied. "Marcus... He... Damn it, I don't know what to make of it."

"Make of what? I can't decipher boys unless you actually give me some information."

I exhaled heavily. "Okay, well we were just hanging in the basement. Mom was out and we were studying. Anyway, Marcus told me that I was beautiful. Marla, I am going to *kill* you if you put him up to this."

The line went silent for a moment. "He said you were beautiful? That's *totally* not him. I thought the only thing about women that interested Marcus was their genetic code."

"Please tell me you put him up to this because I really think that I hurt his feelings with the way I reacted."

Marla snorted. "I didn't put Marcus up to anything. Jules, if he thinks you're all that, you need to put a stop to it right now because one thing I know is that he deserves better than to be strung along."

"I'm *not* stringing him along!" I almost shouted in the phone. "He just blurted it out. God, if he had put the moves on me I don't know what I would have done."

The line went silent again and then Marla said, "Well, are you into him?"

There it was; the unanswerable question.

It's not like I have guys tripping over each other to ask me out. I mean, I know that I'm not drop dead gorgeous, but I *am* pretty. Boys just hadn't been a priority for me and it's entirely possible that I give off a vibe that says as much. For all I know, that alone could be the reason nobody has ever actively pursued me. I'd just always assumed that Marcus was content to remain in the friend zone because as a rule, he scoffs at all the drama associated with dating and first kisses and ugly break-ups. It's not like he's unattractive, either. Marcus has soft green eyes and he doesn't have a dorky voice. He's skinny but he wears it well – or he would wear it well if he updated his wardrobe. But was I into Marcus? To be honest, I'd never once put a moment of thought into the prospect of our becoming an item.

But Marcus *is* good.

He doesn't have an agenda that involves playing head games with girls or anyone for that matter. He's honest to a fault and he genuinely wants to do the right thing – his moral compass is always bang-on. He doesn't wear pants that hang down past his ass and he doesn't try to mimic the style and fashion of a rapper or pop star to get a girl's attention because he's comfortable in his own skin. Hell, he's probably the most self-confident person I know and he's done right by me since the day I met him.

And if he was genuinely expressing a romantic motive when we were down in the basement, I badly misread it and probably humiliated him in the process.

Oh, Marcus, I really, *really* suck.

I gripped my cell phone tightly and banged it into my forehead.

"Jules? Are you still there?" asked Marla.

"Yes," I said, sounding wholly contrite.

"So… are you *into* Marcus Guffman?"

I let out a huge sigh and finally said, "I don't know… *maybe?*"

I didn't get much sleep and like most people, when I'm tired, I get cranky and pissed off at the smallest of things. And some things not so small, like jerks at Crescent Ridge High School who daily spot the invisible target on my nerdy best friend's forehead and make his life a living hell.

That's how my Monday started, actually. I'd just

closed my locker door when I heard a loud metallic *clang* along with a pathetic sounding groan coming from down the crowded hall. I pushed through the throng of students until I spotted a Crescent Ridge Eagles football jacket on a very large and very involved looking jock whose IQ is in the single digits. Oh, and Marcus was in there somewhere because I spotted his skinny legs sticking out of a trash can like a pair of denim-covered chopsticks. His backpack had been ripped open and his homework was spread out all over the floor along with his textbooks.

The culprit? Why, it was none other than Mike Olsen, Crescent Ridge's star defensive back. At six foot two, with perfectly manicured black hair framing a chiselled face with sharp cheekbones and piercing blue eyes that can glamour most females better than any vampire, Mike is a physical specimen best suited for steroid advertisements. He's also a class-A jerk who started picking on Marcus in grade five and hasn't let up ever since.

Okay, I *might* have actually had something to do with Mike's hate-on for Marcus when I slipped the goon a potion that basically gave him a mild form of dysentery, this after he humiliated Marcus at the school convocation last year. Marcus was called up onto the stage to accept an award for academic achievement and Mike Olsen felt that it was important to cough out the world "loser" loud enough for everyone to hear. This led to most of the students joining in and Marcus was laughed off the stage.

That and I kind of stood outside Mike Olsen's bedroom two nights later to watch him screaming hysterically after I guided a harmless chaos spirit through his window. Mike has his suspicions about me but he'd never dare admit them in a thousand years because to do so would be insane for someone so popular. So yeah, the guy bugs the hell out of me and I hate that Marcus can't stand up for himself because he'd get his skinny ass handed to him if he were ever to try.

"You don't look like you've had a healthy breakfast today, Guffman," Mike taunted, as he opened a small carton of milk. "Maybe a shot of two percent will help those brittle bones of yours along."

"Jerk," I muttered as I made sure nobody was looking. I gathered my magic and whispered a tiny spell. "*Hexus.*"

The small carton of two percent burst open in Mike Olsen's hand sending a bone white spray of milk up into his eyes and all over the front of his coveted Crescent Ridge Eagles jacket.

"Son of a…" Mike snarled, baring his teeth. "What the hell?"

A crowd of twenty or so students stepped back as Mike spun around and glared at me.

"You!" he hissed.

I pointed my index finger into my chest and mouthed the words, "Who, me?"

Mike's eyes narrowed as the milk dribbled down his cheeks and onto his t-shirt. "There's something not right about you and Guffman, *freak*! It's the worst-kept secret at school."

I clenched my jaw as I glanced at Marcus who was struggling to climb out of the trash can and then flashed a menacing look at Mike.

"You know, Mike," I said taking a threatening step forward. "Freaks can be *very* dangerous people when provoked."

The air crackled with static electricity and the hallway lights flickered for a moment. Magical energy surged through my body and I could feel my pulse throbbing in my temples as Mike stepped back against a wall of Pepto Bismol-coloured lockers. It was everything I could do to stop myself from lashing out at the goon and a large part of me wanted to say the hell with it and just nail him with a hex that would blow him out of his sneakers.

The corner of his mouth twitched and he took a nervous look around at the growing crowd of spectators. Marcus calmly collected all of the loose leaf paper that was scattered around the trash can and stuffed it in his backpack.

The giant football player's lips curled up into a thin smile as he squared his shoulders and flashed me a contemptuous glare.

"Oh... *now* I get it," he said in a mocking tone. "You're *totally* into Guffman. Now everything makes perfect sense."

I stomped up to Mike and dug my index finger in his chest. "This is getting boring, Mikey... what is it now, the *eighth* time in the last month that you've either stuffed Marcus in a garbage can or locked him in a girl's bathroom? Talk about *stalkerrific*."

Mike nervously looked around at the crowd who were whispering amongst themselves and clearly waiting for a face-saving comeback. He huffed a few times and all he could manage was a benign sounding "*What*?"

"Listen, Mike… it's totally cool if you're into Marcus, okay? I mean, it's gotta be the reason for why he's always on your radar. I guess you stuffed him in the trash because Marcus doesn't feel the same way? Look, nobody is going to judge you – we're all about being supportive of alternative lifestyles here at Crescent Ridge."

Mike was speechless. His face had turned near crimson and he clenched his fists together so hard that his knuckles turned white. Had it been a guy who'd pushed his buttons about Marcus, there would have been an all-out bone-shattering scrap of epic proportions, but I'm a five-foot-two redhead with a short temper. He wasn't about to take a swing at me, and both he and I knew it.

"Get away from me, *freak*!" he roared, as he brushed my hand aside and pushed through the crowd of onlookers.

I unclenched my fists and was just about to help Marcus collect his textbooks from the floor when I saw that I'd been beaten to it by Marla.

What can I say about Marla Lavik? Well, being a Goth, she makes it well known that she has a pretty depressing take on life. I don't entirely understand the Goth culture or the need to dress like a vampire, but I do know one thing about her: Marla has a body that basically every girl at school would kill for. Sometimes I think that's why she dresses the way she does – to get the boys looking and to get their girlfriends fuming.

Today Marla was clad in a tight-fitting, long-sleeve black latex top with laces in the front, and around her neck she wore a spiked choker. There was a thin silver chain that stretched from the piercing in her left nostril to the black stud in her right earlobe and she had bitch boots that came up to her knees complete with six inch spiked heels. She calmly piled the textbooks in her arms and handed them to Marcus.

"Thanks, Marla," he said quietly.

"Don't sweat it," she said, adjusting a bat-shaped comb in her inky black hair. "You know, I totally get what it feels like to be the target of harassment. I mean, at least I used to. I took some steps to keep it from happening in the future and after today, I think that you should too."

"Hey, Marla," I said, purposefully butting in on their conversation. "Nice outfit?"

I felt the tiniest twinge of her spirit flickering to life as she cocked her head and threw me a thin smile.

"Jules," she purred, eyeballing me from head to toe. She reached over and snagged a single strand of my hair from my blouse, examined it and then rolled her eyes. "You know, we really should hit up the mall sometime... there's nothing wrong with a little shock and awe in your choice of hairdos, not to mention your wardrobe. Did you um… address that *thing* we talked about?"

I threw Marcus a nervous look and then I turned my eyes to Marla's killer boots. "I'm still working it out. Where the hell did you get those?"

She waved a hand. "The boots? I used the power of parental guilt on my dad. They cost like five hundred bucks. Having divorced parents who hate each other can do wonders for a girl's walk-in closet."

"I can't afford to even look in your closet," I said sourly. "So, you used to have close encounters with morons like Mike Olsen?"

"Once upon a time I did," she said, with a slight edge in her voice. "But I learned how to manage the assholes of the world. Marcus, you really should learn to take matters into your own hands, otherwise idiots like Mike Olsen are going to keep pushing you."

He stuffed his textbooks into his backpack. "I'll take that under advisement, Marla. I think the safest bet for me is to sharpen my efforts at remaining an anonymous entity at school."

She scribbled into a notepad with a black paisley cover and tore out a tiny sheet of paper. "Well," she said as she casually stuffed the note into Marcus' breast pocket. "Anytime you want a little insight into how to keep it from happening in the future, text me. Jules, what we talked about? You really should do the right thing."

Marcus blinked. "What thing?"

"It's nothing!" I blurted out. "Girl stuff that has to do with clothes and makeup and hair and–"

Marla glanced at her watch. "And I have precisely three minutes to make it to chemistry. Marcus, text me, okay? Jules, TTYL okay? Ta!"

"Ta-ta," I said, burying a sudden pang of jealousy. What the hell was Marla doing giving Marcus her phone number? The pang of jealousy suddenly morphed into a form of mild panic. What if he texted her and she spilled the beans about our talk last night? What if Marcus discovered that I was trying to sort out my feelings? I already felt like the biggest ass in the universe having embarrassed my best friend, the last thing I needed was for that same friend to learn from my girlfriend what I couldn't tell him myself! What would he think of me then?

Marcus heaved his bulky backpack off the floor and I grabbed the shoulder straps as he slipped it onto his shoulders.

"I gotta learn to keep a lower profile," he said quietly.

"Marla gave you her number. What was *that* about?" I asked, mildly annoyed.

"Beats me," he said, examining her note. "She probably wants me to help her study for midterms."

"Or she's into you," I said, surprised by my reaction.

"Me and Marla?" he chuckled. "Well, I'll admit that she's what the higher mortals describe as smoking hot, but Marla is a bit on the extreme side for me. I mean she has a tattoo of a scorpion on the back of her neck for crying out loud!"

I allowed myself a moment to exhale in relief.

"You know," I said, glad that Marcus wasn't attracted to Marla, "maybe she wants to give you a Goth makeover as payment for helping her with midterms – though I'm pretty sure it'll kill your mom when she sees you've turned to the dark side."

"Ha-ha," he said sourly.

I blinked. "So what precipitated Mike Olsen's affections this time?"

Marcus shrugged. "My very existence, I guess," he said quietly. "Thanks for the help, Julie, but this shit is going to continue. What just happened probably made it worse, actually."

He was right.

Mike Olsen wasn't about to slap around a girl, and since he'd been properly dressed down by yours truly, it meant that he'd be gunning for Marcus despite my threats. In defending Marcus, I'd embarrassed the meathead in front of a group of students and there was just no way in the world he was going to be fine and dandy with anything he'd view as a blight on his popularity.

I walked with Marcus to his physics class and said little because I knew that deep down inside, he really wished he could stand up for himself. I mean, he'd be fine if a confrontation were on his terms, like a debate on physics or math. Unfortunately High School isn't about academics and the search for truth despite what our teachers say, so it was pretty clear my intervention just dropped Marcus down a few more notches despite my best intentions.

"Are we still on for the Beltline?" I asked.

Marcus slid the backpack off his shoulders. "Yep. I'll meet you at your locker after school and we'll take it from there."

"See you then," I said.

Marcus disappeared into his classroom and I walked through the second floor foyer leading to my first-period math class. It was time to do that calculus exam.

Or so I thought.

No sooner had I passed the large glass display case filled with Crescent Ridge High School's academic awards when I felt a series of thin jolts charge the atmosphere inside the foyer. I instinctively stopped dead in my tracks and held out my left hand. I shut my eyes and spread my fingers wide open, increasing my focus in the hope of determining the source. It felt eerily similar to the stew of energy at Mrs Gilbert's house, and just as before, I didn't sense any menace but there was something different about it. Like when you take a sip from a half-full bottle of cola that has been sitting in the fridge for a few days. It still tastes like cola, but the fizziness is gone.

Students brushed past me on their way to class, drifting through web-like tendrils of energy like a warm breeze blowing through the leaves on a tree. I grated my teeth together and drew my focus into a dome of magic, and then I whispered, "*Reveal.*"

The artificial light in the foyer dimmed as I opened my eyes and peered through the magical veil. I could see vaporous lines of spectral energy woven together in an intricate pattern that clung to the ceiling and drooped down the foyer walls like the curtains in an opera house. Students appeared as faint shadows, their auras muted by a rhythmic pulsing of grey-green light that coursed along the ceiling and down the walls.

I'd never seen anything like it before. Most supernatural energy emanates from a single source, usually a spirit that appears or disappears, often within the blink of an eye. What I was witnessing was a complex pattern of energies that implied a purpose, but what? Why the second floor foyer of a high school?

My instincts told me to somehow interact with whatever I was seeing, but there was no way to do it in a bustling foyer full of students on their way to their first class of the day. I didn't know how long the apparition would last and the kind of interaction I was thinking of would take time, intense concentration and a little bit of luck.

The sound of the first period bell cut through my focus like a jackhammer and my dome of magic disappeared. I could still feel the energy surrounding me and I decided that a decent grade on a calculus exam had to take priority. I let out a huge sigh, adjusted my backpack and plodded down the hall to my classroom.

Stupid calculus.

## Chapter 8

I was going to fail the calculus exam because I was distracted.

Guilt generally has that effect on me.

I felt like shit for embarrassing Marcus back at my house when he opened up about his feelings, but the guilt was just the after-effect of not knowing if I liked him the way he liked me. Added to this was the fact that in a few hours we'd be heading out to the Beltline. What was I supposed to do if Marcus decided to make a second attempt? Or worse, what would happen if he put his version of the moves on me? I'd already humiliated him once, and I didn't want it to happen for a second time. He deserved to know if I felt the same way; the only problem was that I needed time to think it through.

And, I'll admit it, I'd probably have to ask Mom for help on this. Ugh.

I'd just finished the second page of the bubble test (you know, the ones where you have to colour in the little multiple choice bubbles with an HP pencil) when

I felt a slight supernatural ripple. I glanced down at my calculator and saw the LCD screen blink once, and then random numbers started appearing and disappearing, as if unseen fingers were punching the keys. I sat very still for a short moment as the same presence I'd felt in the foyer seemed to expand in size like a balloon that was being inflated.

"What the hell?" I whispered. I looked up at the clock above the whiteboard and saw the hands spinning backward, as if the same unseen fingers that were messing with my calculator were now turning their attention to unwinding the clock. Just then, an almighty crash that sounded like a head-on collision blasted through the hallway. Everyone in the classroom jumped in their seats and turned their eyes to the door as Mr Dawson, my math teacher, leaped off his turquoise stool and raced for the exit.

"What!" he gasped, as he stuck his head through the doorway and peeked out at the hall. "Impossible!"

The entire class dropped their pencils and headed to the door, forcing Mr Dawson into the hallway. I pushed through the crowd and when I saw what everyone was gaping at, my jaw dropped.

Every single locker on both sides of the hall had been turned *upside down.*

I gulped as I watched students from the adjacent classrooms pour through their respective doorways and into the hall. Amid the gasps and collective profanities, I sensed a presence. A big one.

I forced myself through a wall of dazed and dumb-struck students, and back to the foyer to find the glass display cases turned flipped over and the collection of academic trophies apparently defying gravity as they too were upside down instead of, you know, lying in a heap of broken glass and metal. I grunted as I stuck out my hand to feel the spectral energy pulsing away like a ticking time bomb. A stab of panic raced through the pit of my stomach so I dashed through the foyer to the east wing of the second floor and gulped again when I saw every locker stacked up on their sides like giant coloured building blocks.

"Jesus!" I whispered. "What kind of freaking poltergeist is this?"

I fumbled through my purse and grabbed my cell phone. Within seconds, Mom was on the line.

"You're supposed to be in class, Julie," she said. "Is everything okay? Are you sick?"

I tried to compose myself. "Mom, there's something huge going on at the school. Every locker is either upside down or stacked up on its side. There's a massive web of spectral energy in the foyer and everyone including me is *seriously* freaked out by this."

There was dead air for a second and then my mom said, "Get everyone out of there *now!*"

"What do you think it is?"

"I have no idea but that kind of interaction with the mortal world spells trouble with a capital 'T'. They need to evacuate the school immediately. I'll be there in fifteen minutes."

There was a hint of panic in my Mom's voice and that *never* happens. Naturally it scared the living shit out of me way more than the lockers or the spectral energy because Mom has dealt with supernatural phenomenon a lot longer than I have. Very simply, if it freaked Mom out then it *had* to be dangerous.

If I was going to get everyone out of the school then I'd have to act fast. I tore down the hall until I spotted a fire alarm switch between two stacks of toppled lockers. I clenched my jaw and whispered, "*Hexus*". A bright orange shower of sparks flew out of the red and white switch, bouncing across the floor and the school fire alarm beeped so loud I could feel it in my fillings. Instinctively, all the students in the hall immediately began shoving one another to the nearest door. I spotted Marcus about to be run over as he bent down to pick up his backpack, so I ran interference between two head bangers and grabbed him by the collar.

"Follow me," I ordered. "Take my hand and don't let go."

The presence I'd felt only moments earlier was bearing down on the school like a smart bomb. I could see the east exit leading to the teachers' parking lot amid the huge gaggle of students and text messaged our location to my mom with one hand.

"Poltergeist again, huh?" Marcus shouted in my ear.

"Yes!" I shouted back. "A poltergeist from the

blackest depths of you-know-where. My mother is on her way here."

"They'll be talking about those lockers for months! Good luck to whoever tries to explain this one away!"

I closed my cell phone and stuffed it back in my purse. "They won't be able to. This was a massive display of paranormal activity and I have to tell you, I'm beyond scared."

It was at this point that Leila Belway, Crescent Ridge High's head cheerleader, came screaming out of the girls washroom, knocking me into a water fountain.

"Everybody get out!" she shrieked, mascara running down her cheeks. "Oh my God, there's a dead guy in the girl's washroom!"

The crowd of students spun around and stared at Leila for about two seconds and *that's* when panic really set in. Everyone in the hallway started shouting and screaming as the mob pushed forward in a mad dash to the east exit. Marcus grabbed me by my backpack and yanked me into the alcove of the girls' washroom just in time to keep me from being trampled to death. Seconds later, the temperature inside the hallway spiked up about twenty degrees as a wave of energy poured through the overheated corridor and I doubled over clutching my stomach.

"Julie!" Marcus shouted, as he caught me before I did a face plant into the wall. "What's wrong? Are you okay?"

I shut my eyes tight as I gasped for air. "The spiritual energy in this building is laced with menace! I can feel its hatred, Marcus!"

"We need to get out of here now!" he choked, as he helped me to my feet. "Are you okay to walk?"

I opened my eyes to see the painted cinder block wall in front of me begin dripping ectoplasm in thin sticky threads that pooled at my feet. I tried to focus and could hear teachers were shouting for order but none of the students trying to escape from the building paid them any attention.

And that's when I heard someone calling out from inside the girls' washroom.

"Can you hear that?" I said, leaning on Marcus for support.

"Yeah – someone's stuck in there," he said worriedly.

I spun around on my heels and placed my left hand on the washroom door. "This is a targeted attack, Marcus. Ground zero is behind this door."

"What do we do?"

I could have grabbed one of the teachers but there would have been nothing they could do to help. My instincts told me I should sit tight and wait for my mother, but someone needed our help. I pushed down a tremor of fear in my chest and then reached into my purse and grabbed my amulet. "I'm going to try to get her out. I want you to head for the teachers' parking lot and find my mother."

"Not a chance," he said, shaking his head. "If you're going in there, so am I."

I wasn't going to argue because when Marcus digs his heels in there's no reasoning with him. I chewed my lip for a moment as I palmed my amulet. The atmosphere inside the alcove hummed with a supernatural force that raised the hairs on the back of my neck. The near-deafening beep of the school fire alarm stabbed at my brain like an ice pick, and I gave my head a hard shake.

"Get behind me and crouch down," I said firmly.

"How come?"

"We need to get behind a veil," I said, gathering my magic. "We'll hang tight until the hallway clears or one of the teachers is going to spot us."

"Gotcha," he said nervously.

I focused my spirit into a ball of concentration and whispered, *"Abscondus Occultus."*

Magical energies blanketed us in a thick shadow that blended into the darkness of the alcove. I peered out through the veil to see the throng of students pushing one another to the exit doors. I took a deep breath as I intensified my focus. Just as in the foyer, I could feel a percussive throbbing of spectral energy and this time there was a clear sense of purpose behind it. Sparks of supernatural force tantalized my senses and I could smell a combination of garlic mixed with a faint trace of rot, like a compost heap at the height of summer.

We waited in silence until the hallway had emptied of students. When I was certain the coast was clear, I dropped the veil.

"We're alone," I whispered. "You ready to go, Marcus?"

He nodded. "Yep. Let's get whoever's stuck in there."

"Agreed," I said firmly, as I took a deep breath and slowly pushed on the door. We waited a moment and then carefully poked our heads inside to look around.

"No freaking way!" Marcus said.

The temperature inside the bathroom had to be close to freezing as we could see our breath. There was a deafening clattering sound and our eyes were drawn to the four doors on the bathroom stalls that were repeatedly opening and slamming. I was about to step inside when Marcus stopped me.

"Wait a minute," he said, pointing to the farthest stall. "I can hear her."

I listened closely to the muted sobbing of a female voice. "We have to get to her."

Marcus nodded and set one foot through the door. A trash can slid straight across the entrance to block his way.

"Are you alright?" Marcus called out. "We're going to get you out of here!"

The trash can floated about two feet in the air and hovered gently, as if the poltergeist was deliberately toying with us. I raised my magic and whispered the

tiniest of hexes and the trash can immediately dropped
to the floor, landing with a loud clang.

"Are you injured?" I shouted. "I'm going to need
you to make a run for it, okay?" At the sound of my
voice, the slamming doors abruptly ceased.

"I'm afraid to move," the voice sobbed.

"Damn it, Marcus – that sounds like Marla!"

Suddenly, as if someone had flipped Marcus into
superhero mode, he raced into the bathroom. I didn't
have time to stop him, so I ran to where my magical
senses told me the source of the supernatural energy
was coming from – the large mirror above the sinks.
Marcus needed a diversion or he'd wind up in the
same boat as whoever was trapped in the stall.

"*Hexus!*" I shouted, sending a jolt of force that jet-
ted across the tiled floor and straight into the mirror.
Instead of shattering; the mirror absorbed my magical
attack, sending liquid ripples across the glass like those
from a stone being dropped into a pond.

Marcus tried opening the door to the bathroom stall,
but it wouldn't budge. He ran his hand along the painted
steel surface like he was searching for a weak spot and
he took a step backward as he drove his right foot into
the middle of the door. It flew open and he disappeared
into the stall, reappearing seconds later with Marla
Lavik, the Goth queen of Crescent Ridge High School,
hanging from his right shoulder like a sack of flour.

"Back in a flash!" he huffed, as he ran past me. I
doubled back to the doorway and it slammed shut

with enough force to crack the doorframe in about three places. I felt a surge of paranormal energy that nearly took the breath from my lungs, so I span around on my heels, holding my amulet in front of me for protection. What I saw next at least confirmed Leila Belway's hysterical screaming about a dead guy in the bathroom.

Seated on the counter was a wispy vaporous form of a man who looked like he belonged in the era of Charles I. On his head was a tall crowned, slightly conical hat and he was dressed in a doublet with silver dollar-sized buttons. He wore a blank expression as he drew his near-transparent hands to his breast pockets and turned to look at me. "Who are you?" I asked, stepping inside the washroom. The spectral vision cocked its head and gave me a curious look. It slid off the countertop and floated about a foot off the floor, its unblinking eyes fixed on me. I took a tentative step forward and asked again. "What is your name, spirit?"

The apparition's body pivoted in mid-air and then it raised its hand and pointed to the large stainless-steel-framed mirror above the row of sinks. Suddenly, a thick grey vapour billowed out from the sink's drains. The spirit opened its mouth to say something as the cloud formed a thick steamy mist that clung to the mirror like a shadow. It pointed a bony, vaporous index finger at the center of the mirror and then gracefully started to make swirling motions, like it was conducting an invisible orchestra.

Another jolt of cold force pushed through my body as a series of words took form on the mirror's mist covered surface.

*"Has not this present Parliament*
*A Lieger to the Devil sent,*
*Fully impowr'd to treat about*
*Finding revolted witches out."*

And that's when all hell broke loose.

## Chapter 9

No sooner had I read the words on the mirror aloud when the ghost in the girls' washroom floated up to the ceiling and dissolved into a shimmering mist. The doors on the bathroom stalls started slamming into their chrome locking mechanisms so hard the bolts flew off. Then, all four toilets flushed simultaneously as four concentric pillars of cold water shot straight up to the ceiling, splashing down the walls.

"Gross!" I shrieked as I pulled my blazer over my head and stepped back into the bathroom foyer. A shattering sound cut through the noise of the splashing water and I span around to see an empty stainless steel mirror frame with about a dozen or so large shards of glass floating in the air.

"*Oh shit!*" I said, nearly choking on the words. I crouched down into a ball and held my amulet in front of me. I clenched my jaw and directed my magic to form a protective dome of energy as the shards of glass sailed toward me like jagged daggers. They impacted in a series of splintering thuds that flashed electric blue, and tiny fragments of glass collected at my feet.

Suddenly all three bathroom sinks started shifting up and down, the invisible force trying to tear them from the tiled wall. I had about ten seconds before they'd be transformed into fifty-pound projectiles and I knew there was no way my magic could protect me. The ceramic tiles shattered and crumbled to the floor and more water poured out of the broken pipes in the wall. I grabbed the cold steel door handle and pulled with all my might, but it wouldn't budge, so I did the only thing that came to mind: I raced across the bathroom and dove through the cold, disgusting toilet water, sliding underneath the bathroom stall Marla Lavik had been trapped in. I got to my feet and turned around to see a pentagram, scorched into the tiles behind the toilet.

*"What the hell?"* I gasped.

Suddenly there was an explosion of noise and a cloud of plaster dust filled the air, clogging my nostrils. I could barely see through the powdery white haze as I hunched down on the toilet seat, my body drenched by the cold water pouring up the wall and I braced the door with my feet. I grated my teeth together and willed every last ounce of magic into my amulet, enveloping me in a bubble of energy. The three sinks sailed into the door, sending me careening off the toilet and crashing into the wall behind me.

The coppery taste of blood filled my mouth, the force of my collision with the wall had caused me to bite my tongue, and I cursed in a spray of bloody saliva as I shook my head to clear it.

I could hear pounding on the bathroom door and Marcus' panicked voice.

*"Julie, are you okay? Just stand back, I'm going to try and break through the door to get you!"*

"Don't try to come in here, Marcus!" I shouted back, ignoring my throbbing tongue. "Just go find my mom!"

"Not a chance!" he bellowed. "I'm coming in after you!"

The door thumped loudly as Marcus threw his weight against it in an attempt to break through. I frantically scanned my brain for a quick protective spell just as the toilet beneath me began to shake violently. I could hear a grinding sound as a tremor rolled through the floor. It was at this point I realized the poltergeist, having been unsuccessful at killing me with shards of broken glass and three fifty-pound sinks, was intent on pummelling me to death with the toilets.

Not exactly the classiest way to go.

"I gotta get out of here," I snarled. I dove onto the floor and scrambled out from underneath the stall. The floor pitched violently as I tumbled forward, I could hear the toilets being ripped from the floor so I raced as fast as I could to the furthest corner of the bathroom.

Just then, there was a blast of white-hot energy as the bathroom door exploded into splinters no more than fifty feet away from me. Smoke and dust filled the air as a much stronger magical signature entered the girls' washroom, and I could tell from the way it tingled against my skin that it was really angry.

"Julie Richardson, get your butt out of this bathroom right now! Marcus, stay in the hall!"

I could make out my mom's silhouette through the splashing water and dust, her hands glowing white with magical energy.

Ticked off would be an understatement to describe the tone of her voice and I was probably going to be grounded until my wedding day but it didn't matter. I let out a huge sigh of relief as I scrambled across the slippery bathroom floor and dove out the door for the relative safety of the hallway.

And that was when I witnessed the difference between a novice witch and an experienced practitioner who was in "mother bear protecting her cubs" mode.

"*Filmus!*" she roared, as she sent a blast of magical force from her glowing white hands that roared straight into the ceiling. The floor shook as I staggered up to Mom and stood beside her to see an enormous vaporous orb descend from the ceiling.

"What's that?" I coughed.

Mom didn't take her eyes off the orb. "It's whatever was trying to kill you," she snapped. "And just so you know, what you just experienced in this bathroom is *nothing* compared to what's going to happen to you when we get home."

Oh yeah, *definitely* grounded until my wedding day.

The orb hummed and crackled as my mother's

magic contained the spectre. She reached into her pocket and strolled with confidence to the wall above where the sinks used to be. She drew a large white circle and stepped back. She reached into her purse and pulled out a glass vial containing an oily liquid. She coiled her arm back, drew up her left knee to her chest and then pitched the vial into the center of the circle. It shattered on impact, spraying the oily liquid all over the wall, then Mom calmly walked up to the chalk circle and whispered a word of magic.

"Whatever just happened here wasn't a poltergeist," she said, eyeballing the chalk circle. "Now step back because we're about to be exposed to the torment of all the spiritual energy inside that construct being drawn to the circle. When it contacts the blessed oils I threw at the wall, it will leave the mortal plane and fall upon whoever sent it here."

She was right. This was no poltergeist – it was an assassination attempt.

"I release you," my mother whispered. The orb dissolved in a shower of white sparks. It struggled in mid-air as a roil of spectral energy flew out of the chalk circle. I gaped as I watched a series of wretched-looking faces appear and disappear from within the orb, their hollow eyes and silent, screaming mouths opening and closing, as if bellowing their torment or gulping for air. The wall sizzled, sending tiny plumes of blue smoke up to the ceiling. An unearthly scream filled my ears and a wave of nausea gripped me, forcing me to my knees.

I held my hands over my ears as the scream filled the hallway, causing the flipped over lockers to shake, and then two very clear, bone-chilling words filled the air:

"Endless night!"

A deafening, mournful wail filled my ears followed by a blinding flash that turned the interior of the girl's washroom photo-negative. A gale-force wind blew through the doorway, sending me sprawling across the hall. Mom tried to stand her ground as a tidal wave of heat blasted her, followed by an electric-blue ball of compressed force that shot out and hit Mom in the face, snapping her neck back violently.

"Mom!" I screamed. I watched in horror as her body sailed through the air and crashed into the wall behind me. Another jet of wind blew through the entrance, lifting me off my feet and tossing me into the corner like a discarded toy.

Marcus rushed to my mother's aid. I reached into my pocket and grabbed the copper amulet. I clenched my jaw tightly as I gathered every ounce of focus I could muster and shaped it into another dome of protective energy. One of the bathroom stall doors that had helped protect me from the flying sinks from hell cut through the air like a giant rectangular Frisbee. It smashed into large splinters of broken plywood and painted sheet metal as it crashed against my protective shield. My amulet burned inside the palm of my hand and I shut my eyes tightly, summoning an almost primal level of power I'd never thought existed within my magic.

I stood up and struggled over to the doorway, becoming enveloped in the supernatural energy. Ectoplasm poured over my body in a shower of chilled slime and dripped onto the floor.

I shrieked with rage. *"Begone whoever the hell you are! I command you leave this place!"*

The cloud of energy swirled violently. I ground my teeth together and thrust the amulet out like a battering ram.

*"Begone!"* I roared.

Amazingly, at the utterance of my command, the tornado of energy disappeared into the chalk circle with a lingering hiss. I dropped to my knees as I tried to catch my breath, and then I glanced over my shoulder at my mother.

Marcus was kneeling over my mother with a terrified look on his face. I went to them, hunkered down and gave her a hard shake.

"Mom? Are you alright?"

She didn't move.

*"Mom?"*

Marcus ran a shaking hand across her right cheek and whispered, "She's ice cold."

## Chapter 10

The ambulance arrived within twenty minutes and the doctors confirmed Mom was in a coma three hours after that.

This was my fault.

I leaned on Marcus as we sat in the private waiting room of the intensive care unit at Rockyview Hospital. It reeked of antiseptics. I was numb all over and I barely noticed the heavy-set woman, Ms Iverson, from social services kneeling down in front of me.

"Where's your father, Julie?" she asked in a sympathetic voice.

"He's gone," I whispered, my throat was raw from sobbing for the past three and a half hours.

"Gone... You mean your parents are divorced?"

"He's dead," I said shaking my head. "He was killed in a car accident when I was four. I barely remember him."

Ms Iverson took my hand in her sweaty palm and tried a reassuring squeeze. It didn't work.

If only I'd decided against going back into the school. If only I'd just waited outside for Mom like she asked, I'd be at home studying calculus while she was in the kitchen making supper. As if he'd been reading my thoughts, Marcus leaned in and whispered in my ear.

"Don't blame yourself, Julie. Your mom knew what she was doing and there's just no way to have foreseen this. You have to know that she took every precaution."

I slumped against his shoulder. "But it *is* my fault," I sniffled. "I screwed up. I should have got out of the school and waited for her to show up, but I wanted her to finally see what I could do, that I didn't need her being so over-protective all the time. Now she's hooked up to a bunch of tubes and machines."

I ran through the facts in my head. What I'd thought was a poltergeist was in fact a spiritual construct. I'd read a creepy message in what looked to be old-fashioned English with a warning that witches were somehow a target. I should have high-tailed it out of there, but I didn't. I was cocky and over-confident and now my Mom was in a coma. She was breathing with the help of a ventilator and no doctor in the world could bring her back because what put her in the hospital couldn't be cured by medicine.

Ms Iverson sat down beside me and flipped a yellow sheet over a pile of other yellow sheets on her clip board. She made a few notes and then clicked her pen and slipped it into the breast pocket of her blazer.

"Julie, is there anyone in your family we can call?" she asked quietly. "Under the eyes of the law, you're still considered to be a minor. If we can't find next of kin, we're going to have to take you away for a few days while a court decides where to place you."

"That won't be necessary," said a stern female voice from the doorway to the waiting room. I looked up to see a portly woman with a pair of cat's eye glasses and thin grey hair pulled back underneath a fake leopard-skin hat.

The social worker stood up and started flipping through the pile of sheets on her clip board. "And you are?" she asked, without looking up.

"I'm Julie's legal guardian," the woman said, whipping out a sheet of paper from her matching fake leopard-skin purse. "Have a look and you'll see everything is in order."

Ms Iverson gave the woman a sceptical glance and snatched the sheet out of her hand. She held it close to her nose and I could see her lips moving as she read the document. The woman with the garish hat and purse waited patiently as I gave her a quick scan. She was dressed in a similar spotted overcoat that looked like it was a throwback to the Fifties. Her black satin gloves stretched up to her elbows and there was an enormous emerald ring with a stone the size of a ping-pong ball on her right ring finger. Her thickly painted lips curled up into the creepiest version of a reassuring smile that I'd ever seen, and I was struck by how her eyes sparkled under the fluorescent lights of the waiting room.

Marcus nudged my ribs with his elbow. "Who's that?" he whispered.

"I have no idea," I said, still eyeballing the woman.

The social worker started jotting down information on her clip board of power and handed the document back to the lady in the cat's eye glass.

"Betty Priddy?" she asked as she scribbled away. "Is that with two d's?"

"That's right," the portly woman said, the smile frozen in place by pounds of makeup.

"I'm going to need an address and contact information," the social worker piped up.

Ms Priddy rolled her eyes and gracefully waved two fingers in front of the social worker's face. Ms Iverson's clipboard slipped out of her hands and landed on the floor with a loud smack.

"You don't need our address and contact information," Ms Priddy said calmly.

The social worker glazed over and I could have sworn I saw a thin line of drool slither out the corner of her mouth.

"I don't need your address and contact information," she said in a monotone.

Ms Priddy's smile broadened. "We'll be staying at Julie's house."

"You'll be staying at Julie's house," the social worker repeated like a robot.

Marcus nudged me again in the ribs, good and hard. "Am I going crazy here or is that lady in the fur doing a Jedi mind trick?"

I nodded slowly as Ms Priddy sauntered over and folded her arms. Her thickly painted smile didn't even twitch as she gazed down at me, then at Marcus and back to me again.

"Julie Richardson and Marcus Guffman," she said thrusting out her hand. "I'm Betty Priddy and I'm just tickled to death to have finally met you."

Marcus slowly rolled his eyes up to Betty's face and reluctantly held out his hand. "Um, hi?" he said nervously.

She shook his hand good and hard and I could tell she must have had a strong grip because Marcus winced for half a second as his arm flopped up and down like a rubber hose.

I glanced at the social worker. She was still standing like a mindless zombie and hadn't picked up her clipboard. "Who the hell are you, lady?" I asked in a weary voice. "Mom never once mentioned anyone named Betty Priddy before."

She sat down beside me and the smile on her face dissolved into a look of compassion. "I'm your legal guardian," she said with a hint of softness in her voice. "A long time ago your mother made arrangements for your care should anything ever happen to her. I'm sorry to have to be here, Julie, but I'm not sorry to have met you finally after all these years."

All these years?

I didn't know whether to bust out bawling again or start cursing up a storm. Mom and I might get on each other's nerves nine times out of ten, but we'd made a pact to *never* keep secrets from each other. So why hadn't she told me about Betty Priddy? I took a deep breath and regained my composure because I was already an emotional train wreck, but I knew my Mom well enough to know there had to be a sound reason why she kept me in the dark.

"Can I see that letter you gave to the social worker?" I asked firmly. Betty nodded and handed me the folded document.

It had the Seal of a Public Notary on the bottom and I recognized my Mom's signature. I scanned up the page and read aloud:

"*Statutory Declaration. I, Donna Regina Richardson of the City of Calgary in the Province of Alberta hereby make oath and say that I am the mother of Julie Elizabeth Richardson. That I hereby name Betty Priddy to be the legal guardian of my daughter. Sworn before a Commissioner for Oaths in the City of Calgary in the Province of Alberta.*"

I handed the document back to Betty and gave my head a hard shake. "She wrote this less than a month after Dad died!" I gasped. "Why?"

Marcus put his arm around me again and I slumped in my chair. My head was swimming with questions and I didn't have the energy or inclination to ask them.

"Your mother made this declaration to protect you, Julie," the strange woman said. "The reason she hadn't mentioned me before is because my presence hasn't been needed until now."

I looked up at her as my eyes flooded with tears. "I saw what you did to the social worker," I said, choking up. "Mom always said that screwing around with people's heads was forbidden. She told me that any witch who did so would face swift punishment."

Betty's painted lips curled up into that creepy looking smile again, and she placed a reassuring hand on my knee.

"That's right," she said softly. "But who said I was a witch?"

Marcus gave her a puzzled look. "If you're not a witch, then what the hell are you, lady?"

Betty squared her shoulders and tugged at her leopard skin coat.

"I'm your tutelary, Julie. And we have a lot of work to do."

## Chapter 11

We were back in my house within the hour. For the first time in my life, I couldn't feel my mother's presence. Sure, I was surrounded by the physical reminders of the home she'd built for both of us: a half-filled coffee pot from the morning's breakfast; my mother's tapestries hanging on the walls leading up the stairs to her bedroom; a large double boiler filled with the disgusting horseradish concoction she'd been making. Everything in our entire home represented my mother and our lives together; but the knowledge that she was no longer just a holler away sliced through the numbness like a machete and told me one cold hard fact: Mom might not survive.

Betty wanted to send Marcus home, but I needed his support. He'd called his parents to let them know Mom was in the hospital and he was going to be staying over to keep me company, God love him. The doctors were mystified by the fact there was no apparent physical injury to my mother that would medically justify why she was in a coma. She was in perfect health and her x-rays showed no trauma, but she was unconscious and unresponsive nonetheless. When they asked me what happened, I had to lie of course. Nobody believes in magic even though it surrounds us every single day. I said she simply "collapsed" at school.

Betty padded into the living room with two steaming hot mugs of tea in her hand – not exactly my beverage of choice when it's a stifling hot evening, but her heart was in the right place. She handed one to Marcus and I took the other without saying a word. She offered a warm smile and then sat down in the armchair opposite Marcus and me.

"You're going to have to pull yourself together, Julie," she said in a gentle but firm voice. "We need to help your mother."

I furrowed my brow as I sipped at the tea. "I'm trying – just hard to focus right now. You said you were a tutelary – what's that?"

Betty nodded. "Tutelary spirit, actually. It's really rather complicated but in a nutshell I'm your guardian and I've borrowed this body in order to provide you with guidance and protection while we figure out what happened to your Mom."

"Borrowed this body?" Marcus gasped. "Well who the hell is Betty Priddy? Whose body are we talking to then?"

"Well Betty Priddy is me, of course. My true name is unpronounceable to your kind, so I concocted this one for whenever I might be needed. The body I am occupying is that of Margaret Somerton, who, until about four hours ago, was suffering from a coronary embolism and quite near death, I'd say."

"I can't believe we're actually having this conversation," said Marcus as he sniffed at the mug of tea. "What kind of hallucinogen did you spike us with? I don't do drugs!"

Betty heaved a weary sigh. "There are no drugs in your beverage. I am what I claim to be and we don't have time to bicker about whether you choose to believe me or not. The legal paper confirms that I'm Julie's legal guardian and we need to focus on helping her mother."

Of course she was right.

I'd encountered all kinds of spirits as part of my training to become a witch, but I'd never heard of animistic spirits before. Not that it mattered what kind of spirit Betty was because they all have one thing in common: they're completely amoral. They don't experience their existence through the veil of human belief and values and that's why Betty was being so nonchalant about acquiring the body of someone who was near death.

"She's just doing her job, Marcus," I said. "Chill, okay?"

Marcus put his mug of tea on the end table and folded his arms across his chest.

"Fine, whatever," he said, scowling at Betty. "Just steer the hell clear of *this* body, lady. Got it?"

I turned my attention back to Betty and said, "So how did you know to show up today? Contacting a spirit usually requires some kind of powerful summoning spell."

Betty shrugged. "I simply knew something terrible had happened. Such was the compact between your mother and I, bound together by pure magic and a promise that should anything ever happen to her, my essence would take form in the mortal realm. I needed a host to contain my essence and since Mrs Somerton was indeed very close to passing on, it made sense to borrow her until all this nasty business of comas and poltergeists goes away."

"And how does my mother know you?" I asked. "I mean, you're a spirit so I'll assume you don't exactly have a mailing address."

"She summoned a tutelary spirit," said Betty with a sniff. "I answered the call."

"That's it?" Marcus grumbled. "She just snapped her fingers and *poof!* There you were?"

"It doesn't work that way," she said with a shrug. "I am here in an advisory capacity only and Julie's mother knew this when she made arrangements for her care in the event of her…"

"Her death?" I snapped. "Might as well say it because that's probably what's going to happen to her."

Betty's features hardened and she stomped her foot on the carpet in frustration. "That's enough!" she growled. "Much is about to happen and none of it good. I answered your mother's call all those years ago because she demanded a guardian who knew the answers but not the questions."

I gave her a helpless look and threw my arms in the air.

"The answers but not the questions? What the hell is that supposed to mean? You're speaking in frigging riddles, for crying out loud!"

"That is what I am bound to in accordance with your mother's will when she summoned me, Julie. I recommend you think good and hard about the nature of my being here. It is entirely possible your mother believes that a natural curiosity exists within you to ask the right questions, and I will happily answer when asked. In short, your mother is confident enough in your intellect that you will find those questions when the time arises. I'm thinking that time is now, wouldn't you agree?"

I was exhausted. My head was swimming with emotions ranging from shock at nearly losing Mom to rage that whatever was responsible for her being in a coma was out there somewhere. I took a deep breath and tried to calm down. I had to remain objective and it was pointless to direct my frustration at Betty because she was doing what my mother had willed her to do.

"Look, Betty," I said trying to contain my frustration. "I'm sorry, okay? You said that a whole bunch of stuff was going down, so I'm assuming that it has to do with whatever put my mother in the hospital. If that's the case, I'll start with the poltergeist at Mrs Gilbert's house. Do you know who or what yanked it into the mortal world?"

Betty shook her head. "I know that a magical presence was tainted with the stench of malice that is benchmark for a very ancient form of dark magic. Mortal practitioners like you and your mother could easily detect the malice but neither of you are sensitive enough to trace its origin."

I blinked at her a few times and then asked, "All right. Is it fair to assume more poltergeist activity is about to occur?"

"I suspect that is the case, yes."

"Then is the poltergeist activity part of some evil plot or something?" Marcus asked. "I mean, why drag a spirit back into the world of the living unless you're going to use it for something pretty nasty? Maybe whoever did it is... I don't know, enslaving the spirits or something?"

Betty flattened her skirt and squared her shoulders. "I don't know of any mortal devices or scientific methods that would contain a spiritual entity's will. No, I think this goes well beyond the realm of alchemy. Use your instincts, Julie. They'll lead you in the right direction."

Great. Not only did Betty pull Jedi mind tricks on people, she actually sounded like Obi-Wan Kenobi.

I chewed my lip for a second and considered what I'd been taught about spirits and the afterlife. Namely, that when a person dies, their immortal soul normally crosses over to what is conventionally called "the other side". The other side is a manifestation of positive energy or negative energy – in other words, heaven or hell. Mom says that how a person's immortal soul winds up in either place is a question that nobody really knows the answer to. Religious people consider it to be a matter of faith whereas good old Marcus hypothesizes there is an after-life pipeline for every single one of us and that the negative or positive influences of our deeds in life will determine what happens when we die. The living energy that fuels our very existence and acts as a force for good goes to the happy place and the negative energy, the spark that ignites the darkness that exists in all human beings… Well, it fuels the bad place. So at the moment of death, Marcus thinks your soul is dragged to whichever locale contains more energy than the other.

In order to pull a spirit back from either domain would require some pretty amazing magic and the ingredient for the spell would have to be enhanced by the power of emotions like jealousy or hate which can provide just the right kick to make a spell deadly.

"My gut tells me that if a spirit was brought back to the mortal plane, then this all has to be part of some larger scheme. Maybe the spirit is being used as part of a spell recipe. I mean, what use is the ghost of someone who's been long dead?"

Betty crossed her legs and a look of mild satisfaction formed on her face. "You're thinking like an experienced witch, I'm impressed," she said. "The answer to that question is staring you straight in the face and the sorry victim is lying in a hospital bed right now."

I shuddered as the truth hit me like a freight train.

"Crescent Ridge wasn't the target. It was just a ruse to so it could go after my mom or me!" I gasped.

Betty's face took on a grim look. "That's right, Julie. Whatever it is, it was aimed at the pair of you. Only you were the bait to force your mother's involvement."

## Chapter 12

I sat, my feet hanging over the edge of my bed. I stared hard at my amulet. I remembered the first time I'd ever seen it, dangling from a thin chain around my mother's neck. Dad had been gone for less than a year and Mom and I had planned a picnic. We were seated on a flannel blanket underneath an enormous poplar at Confederation Park. The sounds of robins and magpies filled the air and the warm, early spring breeze carried the scent of lilacs and freshly mown grass.

She beamed at me. "Raise your magic and you'll feel the tug of energies surrounding all living things, Julie."

"Everything?"

She nodded. "We're all bound together by the energy that flows from our hearts. Every breath you draw, every touch of a loved one's hand – we all glow with these energies from within. The trees, the sunlight, the grass underneath the blanket… The entire world hums with life. If you reach out with your spirit, you'll be able to feel it, sweetheart."

I stretched out a tiny hand that was covered with henna tattoos and spread my chubby fingers wide.

"Like this?" I asked.

"That's right," she said, as her fingertips brushed against mine. "Concentrate now. Clear your mind of all your thoughts and you'll feel the tiniest fragments of living energy."

I shut my eyes tight and pushed all thoughts out of my head. Within seconds I could feel a gentle pulse of energies tingling against my skin; tiny snaps that felt like little jolts of electricity in the warm air.

"It's working. I can feel it!" I gasped.

"I can feel it too, sweetheart. Now open your eyes."

I squeezed the amulet tightly as I fought back the urge to cry, the memory was so vivid that I could still feel the warmth of the sun against my skin, and I wanted more than anything to relive that first lesson in magic with my mother. But I couldn't. I was alone in my room, Mom was in the hospital and I felt completely lost.

I had to do something – anything – to help her.

School was out of the question if I was going to get to the bottom of the attack on my mother. I'd have to scour her thirty or so books on spells and incantations because somewhere there had to be lingering fragments of dark magic that I'd missed. Marcus stayed with me all night and as 7.30am rolled around, I told him that I needed some time to sort myself out and that I'd call him after school. He initially kicked up a bit of a fuss, but I smoothed things over by asking him to keep any eye out for anything supernaturally weird that I should know about. Of course, Principal Eggleston would want to discuss why the second floor girls' washroom was destroyed and why my mother was taken from Crescent Ridge Junior high school in an ambulance, so Betty drove Marcus to school and promised to use her own special set of skills to convince the principal that a water surge had blown through the bathroom's plumbing.

Okay, so having a spirit guardian who can pull off Jedi mind tricks can be handy at times.

I sat up in my bed and stared at the wall in front of me. That ache that I'd been feeling in the center of my chest was still there. I wasn't hungry. I wasn't anything more than still very numb. I just wanted to hide away from the world but I couldn't. I needed to find out what happened to Mom, so I crawled out of my bed just as my cell phone vibrated. It was Marla.

DarkChik: OMG, I heard what happened. I'm sooo sry. L

Jules: Thx

DarkChik: What was that at school?

Jules: Not sure. I can't talk okay?

DarkChik: The place is haunted. No other explanation.

Jules: Probly is. I won't be at school today.

DarkChik: I know. Is your Mom… is it bad?

Jules: Yes. Coma. Docs don't know what to do.

DarkChik: LLL

Jules: Thx. I have a question tho.

DarkChik: What?

Jules: What happened in the bathroom? Did u see a star carved in wall in that stall?

DarkChik: Ya. And some stuff like burned grass. I flushed it because it stank.

Jules: That burned stuff. Was it still warm?

DarkChik: I don't know. Why?

Jules: Not sure. Will talk about it l8tr. Txt me if more weird shit happens.

DarkChik: Okay. Hey is Marcus okay? He totally saved my life. 'Swoon'

"Swoon?" What the hell was *that?* I felt my temperature rise and I fired back a text message that was loaded with anger. Okay, so yeah – it wasn't my most shining moment.

Jules: WTF? You choose NOW to tell me ur into Marcus? WTF?

DarkChik: Every girl wants to be rescued. Hey sry okay? I thought you weren't into him.

Jules: I don't know if I am or not. And anyway mom is in hospital.

DarkChik: No Prb. Sry. But it was kind of hot how he carried me out on his shoulder.

Jules: Yeah. Marcus is hot. I gtg l8tr.

DarkChik: CYA.

Marla Lavik's timing sucked ass. It was good of her to check on me and all, but what the hell was she swooning over Marcus for? She knew I was still conflicted about my feelings. Mind you, I didn't have any claim to my dorky friend so in truth; Marcus was fair game for any girl at school. But *Marla?* Every person with male chromosomes ogled her and secretly fantasized about what she looked like underneath all the shining black latex and white makeup.

Everyone… *except* for Marcus.

Maybe it was because of Marcus' apparent lack of interest that he made Marla swoon. (Of course, a good rescue of the damsel in distress can't hurt either, but still.)

I threw my cell phone across the room and it hit my bedroom door with a loud smack. What kind of rubbish daughter was I? My school was attacked by a supernatural entity that nearly killed me, my mother was lying in the hospital in a coma and I was worried about competition for *Marcus?*

Sometimes I'm an asshole with a capital A.

Betty got back to my place shortly after 10am and we decided the first thing we needed to do was to look for a motive. She followed me down to Mom's lab and started pulling books off the shelf and stacking them on the big table in the middle of the room. I'd brought my laptop with me so I could show her the disturbing video of the dogs on YouTube.

"Betty, can you tell me what that is?" I asked as I clicked pause at the precise moment when the blue orb appeared in front of the windowsill.

She pulled her glasses down to the tip of her nose and tucked her chin to her chest as she scanned the screen. "It's not something that can be explained using non-magical means, that's for sure. What's your gut telling you?"

"A spirit," I said flatly. "It's just showing itself in the shape of an orb as opposed to who it used to be in life."

Betty grunted again. "Doesn't it seem rather contrived for a spirit to present itself in full view of a camera or recording device?"

I blinked at her a few times. "So what you are saying is… This video was staged and the whole thing is fake?"

"Oh it is *definitely* staged," she said. "But what you are seeing before you is not a poltergeist, but rather, a feat of magic. The attack on those dogs is just supposed to *look* like a poltergeist, that's all. In time, you'll hone your skills to razor-sharp precision and you'll be able to spot a fake from a mile away."

"I hope so," I said calmly. "So what do you think it means?"

Betty shrugged as she went back to piling books on the table. "I suspect it means that whoever crafted that spell wanted certain people to understand its true meaning… but not everyone. What is more important, having millions of anonymous people observe what might or might not be a supernatural occurrence or a handful of people who know what specifically to look for?"

I chewed my lip and reversed the video. I brought my face close to the screen and squinted as I clicked play. I watched the curtains flutter and I jumped when I saw a tiny spark of magical energy a split second before the orb appeared.

"Look!" I shouted, as I clicked stop. "You were right! I saw an arc of energy."

"And what does that tell you?" Betty asked.

I thought for a moment and then gasped. "That we're dealing with some seriously twisted practitioner. But if it's the same person behind the attack on the school, I can't see how they'd have been able to do all that without burning up! It doesn't make sense."

Betty nodded. "It's true – there are rules for magic. It's possible this might be a dark coven of some kind. Perhaps a group of witches pooled their collective energy to do this. Either way, we need more information."

I raised a finger. "A broker! We could hit up Holly Penske for information. She's in the know about everything supernatural, though my mother told me that she plays both sides of the fence."

Betty gave me an immediate look of disapproval. "I'd suggest that you forget about even considering contacting her," she said warily. "Holly Penske doesn't play nicely with anyone and you *never* want to be in her debt."

"She deals with desperate people?" I asked.

Betty's eyes narrowed. "Desperate, ambitious, conniving – she makes no distinction. Holly Penske deals with whoever is willing to pay her fee. She can't be trusted because she's only out for herself."

I turned my attention back to the video. No real web traffic according to the number of hits. It was almost as if whoever planted it there meant for it to be seen by whoever was at the receiving end of their dark spell.

"This video was aimed at someone who'd notice."

Betty nodded. "That's right – someone like you."

I clicked on the author's profile to see if I could glean a bit more information about him. A page immediately loaded with the username 'Hudibras' framed in a green box along with a link to subscribe to his YouTube channel. The background contained black-and-white woodblock prints showing people in medieval garb. I scanned the background further and my heart nearly stopped when I saw a faint text by a man with a long beard dressed in a capotain hat poking a tormented looking woman with what looked like a dagger. I gulped as I read the words aloud:

> *"Has not this present Parliament*
> *A Lieger to the Devil sent,*
> *Fully impowr'd to treat about*
> *Finding revolted witches out*
> *And has not he, within a year,*
> *Hang'd threescore of 'em in one shire?*
> *Some only for not being drowned,*
> *And some for sitting above ground,*
> *Whole days and nights, upon their breeches,*
> *And feeling pain, were hang'd for witches*

"Oh my God! That bearded guy," I gasped. "I saw him in the girls' washroom yesterday. This is the same text that spirit wrote on the bathroom mirror!"

Betty shuffled over to me and leaned over my shoulder. "I'm familiar with it and as I recall, it was written in 1678. That man in the picture is someone I've seen before... His name escapes me."

"Whoever it is, they've clearly got a hate-on for witches," I said. "You don't think..."

"That a spectre is the one responsible for attacking you and your mother at school yesterday?" she said, completing my sentence. "Spirits of the departed can't do magic, but the message might hold the key that unlocks a door to a very harsh reality many witches are in denial about."

"And that would be?"

Betty's eyes narrowed again as she pointed to the woodblock prints. "That persecution of witches is very much alive and well in the twenty-first century."

I chewed on Betty's observation for a moment and then remembered that Marcus and I had sent an email to the video's author. I quickly logged into my email account and waited as ten messages downloaded. The familiar chime sounded to tell me that I had mail. Betty hovered over me, her glasses still perched on the bridge of her nose. I scrolled down past a number of spam messages until I spotted the words, 'Your Request' in the subject line. My eyes scanned to the left and I saw the sender's name was Hudibras.

"Maybe the answer is in this email..."

"Julie, *don't!*" cried Betty as she reached for my

hand, but it was too late.

I felt the hairs on my arms standing on end. The temperature dropped like a stone and a foul stench of rotting flesh filled my nostrils.

"What's happening, Betty?"

"Spirits bless us all!" she said.

My body floated about five feet off the floor. Mom's spell books flew off the shelves and danced around me, the pages fluttering as a breeze appeared out of nowhere, sweeping across the top of the table and blowing all of Mom's beakers and flasks to the far end of the room. My laptop began spinning like a top and then it floated up to the ceiling, the screen blinking furiously. Dust fell from the ceiling as a tremendous rumble shook the room. I glanced over at Betty and watched in horror as Mom's shelf toppled over, burying her in a pile of spell books and jars filled with spell ingredients.

The chair beneath me lifted off the ground and I ducked as it flew across the room, narrowly missing my head. The supernatural attack was getting out of hand and if I didn't do something, I'd wind up in the hospital too. I clenched my jaw tightly and raised my magic as I reached for my amulet. It tingled against the palm of my hand as I threw up a dome of magical energy to shield my body from the flying debris.

Betty crawled out from underneath the book-shelf, her eyes blazing with supernatural fury. She furrowed her brow angrily and roared, "Whoever you are, you're not dealing with a novice and this spell ends now!"

In a surprising display of her power, the chair that nearly took my head off slid across the floor until it was directly beneath me. I watched in amazement as all the beakers and flasks that had flown off the table and smashed against the wall reassembled themselves, the tiny glass shards fusing together. The remade vessels drifted back to the table and into neat and orderly rows. The books that were orbiting me like satellites circling a planet sailed back onto the shelves and the breeze disappeared as quickly as it started. I slowly dropped to the floor. My laptop fell into Betty's hands and she allowed herself a satisfied smile as she slid it back onto the table.

"Some people need to remember their manners to their betters," said Betty, in an indignant voice. "We're safe now, Julie."

I lowered my magic as the temperature returned to normal and the stench dissipated. Betty placed her hand on my shoulder and squeezed good and hard. I leaned over to the blinking computer screen to read two words that made my heart sink.

"*Two Days*," I whispered.

*Chapter 13*

"Hudibras was definitely behind everything and the email proves it," I said, examining the message. "The time stamp says it was sent the day before the attack at school."

"Then you're clearly the person that video was meant for," Betty said calmly.

I glanced at my watch. "It's 11.33 in the morning," I said in a frustrated voice. "Hudibras sent that email more than twenty-four hours ago. That means we haven't much more than a day to do *what?*"

Betty shuffled over to Mom's bookshelf and ran her index finger along the spines. "You know what must be done," she said.

I frowned. "Do I? If he's behind what happened at school yesterday, maybe he's planning another attack or something."

Betty grunted. "I think we just survived one, now where *is* that book?"

"What book?"

She pulled out a thick leather-bound volume the size of an encyclopaedia from Mom's bookshelf and dropped it on the table in front of her. It landed with a loud slap.

"Your mother's grimoire – her personal book of magic. Have you started your own yet?"

I shrugged. "Well… kind of. I mean, it's on a flash drive and everything's in Microsoft Word. Do you think you'll find the answer in there?"

Betty flipped through the thick pages like she knew what she was looking for and then slapped her hand down on a page about a third of the way through the book. "There it is!" she announced.

I slid over and squinted at the hand-written entries. Betty's finger pointed to a heading entitled, 'The Nature of the Mortal Soul'.

"'The soul constitutes the binding of the physical aspect of an individual's humanity with the existence of their spiritual self,'" she read aloud. "'Religious scholars believe as a matter of faith, that our human soul departs the body at the moment of death. However, the soul can be torn from the body by means of dark magic, the darkest of which is the spell known as Endless Night where the victim lingers on in a persistent vegetative state until death claims them. Without the soul, a human body cannot survive more than a few days before physical death occurs.'"

"Endless Night," I gasped, as my blood ran cold. "A voice bellowed those words just before Mom was attacked. Hudibras used the Endless Night spell to take Mom's soul. But why?"

Betty closed the grimoire and reached across to hold my hand. I was somewhere between panic and relief if that makes sense. I was terrified that my mother might die, but if her soul had been somehow been taken, then if we got it back she'd recover and everything would be as it was. The big problem though was that we'd have to find this Hudibras guy as quickly as possible. A task that is easier said than done in a city with a million inhabitants, not to mention the fact that time was against us.

Betty took a seat in the big chair again and stretched her legs out. "The word 'Hudibras' – can you look on that machine of yours and see if you can dig anything up? It would save us the drudgery of researching at the library or even contacting your mother's coven."

I spun around in the chair and googled the word "Hudibras". Within seconds I had a page with twenty different links, so I clicked on the first one. A page loaded entitled Project Gutenberg, and there was a link to the name *Samuel Butler.*

"It says here that a poet named Samuel Butler was the author of a satirical poem on Puritanism entitled 'Hudibras' and… Holy cow!"

"What is it, Julie?" asked Betty.

I pointed to the flickering computer screen. "It's the same text I saw on the bathroom mirror yesterday and on the YouTube profile."

Betty squinted over to read the webpage and her faced turned white. "The passage is a commentary on the activities of *Matthew Hopkins*. I knew I recognized that woodcut print on Hudibras' profile, but it can't be!"

"What can't be?" I asked in a half-panicked voice. "Who the hell is Matthew Hopkins?"

She straightened her back and her eyes narrowed. "A troublesome character," she said. "A self-appointed persecutor not only of witches, but thousands of innocent women he accused of witchcraft during the seventeenth century. He took his position so very seriously that he named himself the Witchfinder General of England and he swept the entire nation into a frenzy of fear and loathing toward witches and those accused of witchcraft."

I tried to remember everything I'd been taught about the persecution of witches, and it made my skin crawl. Everyone's heard of the mass hysteria that led to the Salem Witch Trials or that Joan of Arc was accused of witchcraft and burned at the stake, but our modern world has closed its eyes to a tainted past where those of my kind were hunted and killed just for being who they were born to be. I didn't know anything about Matthew Hopkins and I wasn't entirely sure where Betty was going with this. The guy had been dead for over four hundred and fifty years, so what was his connection to a person named Hudibras and what did either of them have to do with poltergeist activity or the attack on my mother? I decided to press Betty for answers.

"Just how old are you, Betty?" I asked.

She seemed surprised by my question and eyeballed me for a moment. "Why do you ask?" I twirled around in my chair to face her. "Well, Mom didn't exactly school me on spirit guardians, but you seem to know a lot about Matthew Hopkins. Were you around back then?"

"Age doesn't apply to those of my kind," she said. "You might say that I've been around as long as time itself and I've witnessed humanity's evolution from primordial slime to your current incarnation."

"So what precisely *are* you?" I asked in a confused voice. "I know that my mother summoned you to be my guardian but that doesn't give me much to work with. You've occupied a dying woman's body, and oh, by the way, I'm sure her family has probably filed a missing person report with the police."

"Piff-paff," she interrupted. "If this body becomes a problem I can always find another. Mortals are dying in hospitals all over the city."

"Okay that's just plain creepy," I said, surprised at her inference that human bodies were on the same level as disposable coffee cups. "Seriously, what are you, Betty?"

"Fine," Betty grumbled. "I'm an immortal soul; an amalgam of a variety of naturally occurring spiritual energy that exists in animals, plant life, the wind... You know what I mean. I've been here since the beginning and I will be here long after your bones have turned to dust."

"Gotcha. And the whole Jedi mind trick thing you pulled on that social worker not to mention what you did after you clicked on the message from Hudibras. Your power is probably off the scale."

She nodded slowly. "Oh, there are others who are far more powerful than me. As for the social worker, well, I didn't perform a magical act; I simply imparted some of my essence to that nasty woman's mind to get a desired result."

I nodded as I slid the map of Calgary out from under my laptop. "Marcus and I used a *pendulata* spell to locate where this Hudibras person possibly lives. You can see the drops landed in a section of town called the Beltline."

Betty hunched over and examined the map. She ran her finger from one drop to the next and said, "You know enough to connect those drops of ink, right?"

I gave her a sheepish look and I could feel my face turning beet red. "I didn't think of that," I said quietly. "Marcus and I were planning on going down to the Beltline yesterday after school and I'd intended to let my natural sensitivity to magical energy lead me to this guy. That was before I knew he'd attacked Mom, though."

Betty snorted. "Good thing you didn't because he would have undoubtedly detected your magical signature and it would be you lying in the hospital right now."

"I know that now," I said, as I reached for a pencil and started drawing a thin line from one dot to the next. When I finished, the lines formed a familiar shape to anyone who knows anything about arcane symbols. The kind of familiar shape that sends a jolt of cold fear straight into the pit of your stomach and makes you want to, I don't know, how about hide under a church pew for a few decades?

"The Baphomet Sigil," Betty whispered, as she put her hand on my shoulder and squeezed.

I nodded slowly as the cold fear in my stomach transformed into full-fledged panic.

"The Left Hand Path," I said with a shudder.

Oh yeah. Way over my head.

## Chapter 14

We went to the hospital to check in on Mom and upon our arrival Betty made a beeline to the cafeteria. Apparently even spirits needed sustenance. Food was the last thing on my mind so I wandered up to the intensive care ward and within minutes I was standing in front of Mom's hospital bed. The inhuman sounding hiss of the ventilator along with the high-pitched beep from the heart monitor filled my ears as I took her hand. Gone was the tingling sensation of Mom's magical signature intermingling with mine; that supernatural bond that all practitioners share had been stripped away leaving only a hollow shell that looked like my mother.

But it wasn't her.

No scowl or smile formed on her face. Her eyes were taped shut and a plastic tube attached to a mouthpiece was fixed between her lips. I watched her chest rise and fall with each gust of oxygen as the crushing weight of guilt pressed down on me.

I had caused this.

I should have done as she'd instructed and simply waited for her to arrive but I just had to take matters into my own hands. Now Mom was paying for my mistake.

I would have done anything to see that familiar look of disapproval in her eyes or to be on the receiving end of a blast of shit because I hadn't listened for like the jillionth time. That's what was supposed to happen when I screwed up; Mom would rip at me with a sharp comment or criticism and we'd have an argument until one of us stormed off.

But not this time.

I gently placed a hand on Mom's cheek and whispered a word of magic stupidly thinking that my magic could somehow kickstart her brain, but nothing happened.

Not a thing.

It was shortly before 1pm when Marla Lavik walked into the hospital room and to her credit, she didn't turn it into a dramatic affair.

Yeah, right.

"I didn't know if I should come," said Marla. She placed a black lace covered hand on my shoulder. "And when I got here the staff gave me a hard time because they didn't want me to scare the patients. Assholes! How is she doing?"

"No change," I said quietly as I squeezed my mother's hand. "You know, she drives me nuts every day and yet I can't imagine my life without her. Now she's probably going to die and–"

Marla put her arms around me and I buried my face in her shoulder. "Don't say that, Julie!" she said firmly. "You just have to believe she's going to get through this. The doctors will figure it out."

I sniffed loudly. "I keep hoping that you're right but the looks on the faces of the nurses tell me a different story."

"I know," Marla replied. "But you just have to hold on, okay? She'd want you to keep hoping, Jules."

I nodded and let out another sniff. I pulled away from Marla and I ran my sleeve across my tear filled eyes. "The doctor said there's no reason that Mom should be in a coma. There's no head trauma, no lack of oxygen to her brain… Nothing."

"Maybe for them it's as impossible to figure out as trying to find a rational explanation for happened at school yesterday, Jules. And what the hell was your mom doing inside the girls' washroom anyway?"

I glanced at Marla through the corner of my eye. I couldn't tell her that it was Mom who told me to get everyone out of the school because it was under a magical attack and that her soul had been ripped out of her body, so I decided to lie. It's not exactly like I had a choice in the matter.

"She was coming to get me because I texted her," I said being careful to observe Marla's reaction. "What's everyone saying about all the lockers and stuff?"

Marla shrugged. "That it was a small earthquake – a tremor. But I'm calling bullshit on that story because the science club posted to their Facebook page something about there being no data from the Faculty of Geology at the university to prove there was an earthquake. All I know is what I saw in that bathroom was real. It was a ghost, Jules. I never believed in ghosts until yesterday."

"I know," I said in a hollow voice. "Thanks for coming, Marla."

She adjusted her latex corset with a sharp tug and then walked over to the other side of the hospital bed. I shifted my gaze back to my mother, not wanting to really talk while at the same time hoping that Marla wouldn't leave. I appreciated the company and anything is better than hanging out with a spiritual babysitter that's occupying a dying person's body. We'd said nothing to each other for a few minutes when Marla decided to break the silence.

And I really wished she hadn't.

"So, Jules," she said carefully. "About that text last night."

I blinked. "What about it?"

She avoided my gaze and shrugged. "Well, all that stuff I said about Marcus. I mean, this is probably the wrong time to be talking about boys."

"You're right, it is the wrong time," I said coolly.

Marla nodded slowly. "Yeah, I guess so. I wasn't thinking about you or what you must be going through. I was being self-centered again. I'm a rubbish friend."

I folded my arms across my chest and raised an eyebrow. "Please don't tell me that you're looking for consolation, Marla. I don't have it in me right now and your timing blows, by the way."

"Because I said that I liked Marcus?"

I flashed a fiery glare. "No, because you're talking about boy stuff when I'm holding a bedside vigil for my dying mother!"

She motioned for me to calm down. "Okay, Jules. I get it. Just chill."

"Fine," I snapped. "Listen, Marla, I'd just like to be alone for a while, okay?"

I could have sworn that I saw a flicker of anger in Marla's eyes as she circled the bed. She opened her arms to give me another hug but I raised a hand and shook my head.

"I'm sorry about your mom, Jules," she said quietly. "Text me okay?"

"Yeah, I'll text you, Marla. Later."

I had little to say to Betty after Marla left, partly because I still wasn't sure about my feelings for Marcus, but mostly because I simply didn't like the idea of another girl pursuing him. I didn't want to talk about my feelings because I didn't even know what my feelings were. This was compounded by the fact that I felt like a total ass for even thinking about romance when my mother was at death's door.

Like, how the hell are you supposed to deal with

this kind of stuff? What's the right way to feel? Under normal circumstances, I'd be able to talk my feelings out with Mom, but that wasn't going to happen anytime soon. And there was no way on earth I'd be opening up to Betty. I needed to focus, so I pushed my encounter with Marla out of my head as Betty and I left the hospital. It was blisteringly hot outside, so I threw on my sunglasses as we walked down the shale-covered path toward Fourteenth Street.

Betty blew her nose and stuffed the Kleenex under her sleeve. "You've said nothing to me since we got to the hospital, Julie. Is everything alright?"

"What do you think?" I said icily.

Just then, my phone buzzed in my purse so I flipped it open. It was a text from Marcus and I was in a bitchy mood.

Great.

HawkingFan: Hi. I'm just getting on the C-Train. R U Okay?

Jules: Yes.

HawkingFan: R U at home? I can come over.

Jules: No.

HawkingFan: ??

Jules: What?

HawkingFan: Nothing. I was just wondering if you were going to use sentences instead of one word answers at some point in this discussion.

Jules: Whatever.

HawkingFan: Where R U?

Jules: Train.

HawkingFan: Okay R U mad at me because I'd like to know what I did wrong given that I've been at school all day. I'm selfish that way.

Oh man. I *was* mad at Marcus. I scrolled up to re-read what I'd written when I realized that I'd gone from bitch to just plain evil in fewer than a hundred characters on the screen. But why was I angry at him? He hadn't done anything wrong. Christ, all he was doing was checking in on me because he was worried and I was treating him like a sack of shit. Once again, I whacked myself in the forehead with my cell phone. Just because I wasn't sure about my feelings for Marcus and that I wasn't crazy about his being on Marla's love radar was no reason for me to be a bitch. I thumbed the keypad quickly.

Jules: Look, I'm sorry okay?

HawkingFan: I know. I'm sorry for snapping at you.

Jules: No. I was a bitch. I deserved that.

HawkingFan: So what's the next move?

Jules: Not sure. Will be at Southland Mall Station at 3. Can u meet me there?

HawkingFan: Yep. TTYL

Jules: TTYL Marcus. Thx.

We met Marcus on the train platform at Southland Mall and I noticed that Marcus' T-shirt had a large purple stain running down the middle of his back. It was clear that Mike Olsen must have decided to exact some revenge after my little encounter with him. Naturally I felt bad about it and I had to stop myself from vowing to throw a hex at Mike's knee whenever the Crescent Ridge Eagles played another football game. Marcus seemed to have taken it all in his stride. Maybe after so many years of being pushed around, he'd become desensitized to it.

And naturally I felt like a shit to the power of a million for dumping on him via text.

"So this Hudibras guy is part of something called the Left Hand Path, huh?" asked Marcus as we entered the train. I sat down on a graffiti covered seat and Marcus slid in next to me. "This is getting more dangerous by the moment. Who are these guys anyway?"

Betty took her seat across the aisle from us; her leopard skin outfit was wrinkly from having been worn for two days straight and I noticed her pallor had taken on an almost greyish tone.

"Bad dudes with a hate-on for witches," I said flatly as the train left the station. "Let's maybe keep it down. You never know who might be listening."

Marcus nodded. "Oh, sorry. Look, Julie, your mom is in the hospital – let's just go home, okay?"

I clenched my jaw and dug my fingers into my backpack. "The only thing that matters right now is finding out who attacked her. I need your help on this, Marcus."

"Be patient, Julie," Betty chimed in. "Let your instincts guide you."

Again with the Obi-Wan Kenobi talk! I let out a

weary sigh. I knew that we were dealing with someone whose magical qualities easily surpassed my own, but I had Betty to back me up and a bone to pick with whoever did this to my mother. Of course, dealing with the Left Hand Path presented a host of dangers because if dark magic represents the bad side of town when it comes to witchcraft and sorcery, then the Left Hand Path is the *bad* side of the bad side of town.

Who are they?

First off, there's argument among a lot of religious and philosophical scholars about whether the Left Hand Path is simply a belief system as opposed to, you know, *really* freaking evil people. Just close your eyes and think of the most terrifying experience of your life and multiply it by a jillion or so. They're into everything from human sacrifice to necromancy... Yeah, you heard me, some of these whack jobs actually *raise* the dead! The worst of the bunch worship the Devil himself and are bent on bringing about the end of days, as in the *apocalypse*.

And it was looking like whoever stole my mother's soul was one of them.

We sat in silence for a few moments. The train rounded a corner and came to a smooth stop at the Stampede Station platform. I gave Marcus a gentle nudge. "I'm sorry for dragging you into all this Hudibras stuff. I mean, you've already been attacked and you saved Marla Lavik from likely the same dark magic. I treated you like shit today and I just totally suck at this."

He offered a thin smile and I noticed his eyes softened as he gazed at me. "It's cool, Julie. I've seen all kinds of weird ass stuff as long as I've known you. From what happened in your shed to the time a disembodied voice started a conversation with us during that time when we were ten. Remember that camping trip?"

I snorted. "Yeah, it said it was the spirit of Albert Einstein and it told you the theory of relativity was a sham. You got pretty ticked off about that as I recall."

Marcus chuckled. "Yeah, it tried to convince me that mass and energy weren't equivalent or transmutable – like *that* could ever happen. Anyway, like I said, I'm cool with you sometimes keeping me in the dark. I know you worry my brain might turn into sludge or something with all this crazy stuff going on, but you know what?"

"What's that?"

He beamed at me. "I'm really fascinated by all this, you know? I mean, everything that I've seen since I've known you defies my understanding of science and it's really mind-blowing. I'm actually starting to believe that magic and the supernatural is an undiscovered branch of physics. Maybe it's always been there, you know? Maybe our primitive monkey brains aren't attuned to this stuff and people like you and your mom are possibly the next link in human evolution. I wonder if this fits in with string theory somehow… I'm going to have to make a mental note to research that."

"Marcus," I said softly. "You don't have to come with us for this."

His eyebrows arched. Clearly he hadn't expected me to give him an out. "I've got your back," he said.

"You only saw a part of what happened in the girls' bathroom yesterday," I said grimly.

"I saw the aftermath," he replied. "I saw the ambulance take away your mom and I saw you crying your eyes out at the hospital last night."

"Marcus, there's a reason why Mom's in the hospital and we don't have much time," I said firmly. "While you were at school today, Betty and I pieced together some missing facts from when you and I were looking at that video on YouTube. This is really big, okay? We're dealing with some really serious stuff here."

He waved a hand in protest and his eyes narrowed. "Serious as in something more substantive than an attempt on you and your mom's life?"

"Yeah."

"The Left Hand Path would imply there's a Right Hand Path, am I correct?"

I nodded silently.

"Then I would assume people like you and your mom generally have your feet planted firmly on the right, so that would mean anyone on the Left Hand Path would be like your evil doppelganger or something."

Betty pursed her lips tightly. "And some of those beings would love nothing more than to sink their teeth in you."

"No doubt," said Marcus as he glanced out the window. "Where are we going again?"

The train entered a tunnel and the sound of the steel wheels coasting along the rails roared through the open windows.

"We're going to–"

Suddenly the train lurched, pushing us hard into the seats. The lights went out both inside the train and along the tunnel walls and a shower of bright orange sparks lit up the darkness outside the window as the train ground to a sudden and unexpected stop. My stomach pitched violently as I doubled over, clutching my midsection.

"Julie, are you okay?" Marcus asked in a worried voice.

The two dozen or so passengers started whispering in panicked voices. I reached out with my senses just as an unearthly roar blasted through the tunnel, shaking the car like it was a toy in a child's hand. The roar and the shaking ended and an ominous silence fell on the passengers.

But only for a moment.

"Get your hand off me!" a woman shrieked.

"I didn't do nothing, lady!" a male voice rang out.

The emergency lights flickered for a moment and came to life. What I saw next sent every passenger tearing for the exit.

Dozens of purses and cell phones floated near the ceiling of the car. Jackets and briefcases danced about in the air, as if guided by an unseen force. I heard a cracking sound behind me and ducked as a poster for next year's Calgary Stampede tore off its moorings and sailed into a window, shattering the glass into thousands of tiny cube-shaped pieces. I heard a whooshing sound, and suddenly both sets of doors on the sides of the car nearest the tunnel wall opened. The emergency lights flickered again. The two dozen passengers nearly trampled each other to death in their race to get off the train as quickly as possible.

"Same energy that I felt at the school," I said, still clutching my stomach.

"What do we do?" Marcus said.

Betty got up from her seat looking wholly unimpressed.

"We send it back to wherever it came from. Julie, my powers don't work terribly well if I'm underground. There are fewer living elements from which I can draw on to fuel my magic. If you can detect the source of the energy, there's a chance you can hex it."

My bench seat started shaking and I clutched my amulet as I grabbed Marcus and scrambled to the back of the car.

"I'll give it a try," I said, through stinging tears of pain. "I hope I've got enough in me."

I clenched my jaw and drove my fist into the mass of supernatural fury. Marcus stood up to shield me from the flying debris, his body pounded by everything the passengers had left.

"Just hang tight!" he grimaced as a briefcase sailed into the back of his head. "I've got you covered!"

I wanted to draw another protective dome of energy, but it would keep me from finding the source of the poltergeist activity, so I grated my teeth together and shut my eyes. I reached out with my Sight and saw a haunting liquid-like glow that ran off the walls of the car, forming pools of shimmering malice along the floor. I pushed my senses further, through pure, concentrated hate that threatened to suck the air from my lungs. Then, in the center of the ceiling, I saw it: a throbbing, pulsating blob of energy that bubbled and seethed with a simmering anger that felt as old as time itself. It sensed my presence as I probed for a weak point to direct my hex, and then the unexpected happened.

It spoke to me.

"Being very useful for these times," the voice dripped with menace. "Wherein the Devil reigns and prevails over the souls of poor creatures, in drawing them to that crying sin of witchcraft. I shall not suffer a witch to live!"

A jolt swept me off my feet, sending me tumbling against the back of the car. Marcus raced to my aid but suddenly he was lifted off the floor by his left ankle. He dangled in mid-air for less than a second and then he flew into the wall behind me, with a hard thud.

"Marcus!" I screamed, as I scrambled over to him. "Marcus! Are you okay?"

"Ow," he groaned as he slid onto his side. "I might have said this before, but poltergeists hurt like hell."

It was at this point that something inside me snapped. This was the fourth supernatural assault in two days and twice Marcus had been attacked. I'd exorcised the spirit from the girls' washroom and I'd be damned if some witch-hating piece of crap was going to try and steal Marcus' soul, or mine for that matter.

I strode up to the middle of the car as Betty looked on. I held out my left hand and spread my fingers until I knew I was directly beneath the spot where the entity spoke those menacing words. I held my amulet over my head and invoked the strongest banishment spell I could think of.

"I am a witch of ancient lore," I roared. "And this is the twenty-first century. You want a piece of me, come and get some!"

The car started shaking again and I grabbed a hand hold to keep myself from falling flat on my face. The floating debris which moments earlier had been pummelling poor Marcus flew straight up and crashed against the ceiling.

"Begone!" I cried.

A vaporous mass took form above my head, dripping spectral ooze down my forearm and onto my shoulders. I pushed my amulet into the slushy mess, willing my magic into my banishment spell. It twisted and churned as it tried to resist my power so I drew from my spirit further, digging as hard as I could for every ounce of energy I could muster. A shriek of rage roared through the car as I cast the presence back onto whoever had sent it here. My hair blew in every direction as a stinking breeze swirled around me. In seconds the mass dissolved into a harmless mist and I dropped to my knees exhausted.

Betty strode up to me clapping her hands. "Well done, Julie! That was a remarkable show of will."

"T-thanks," I panted. "You guys okay?"

Marcus slowly got back to his feet and brushed himself off. "Yeah, I'm good. Are we going to head out to the Beltline?"

"The hell with this!" I growled, knowing that where I wanted to go wasn't going to fly with Betty, but I was desperate. "I need an edge if I'm going to end this crap and save my Mom."

Betty folded her arms and gave me a stern look. "This had better not be what I think it is."

I shot her a defiant glare. "Yeah, Betty, it is – we're going to Bankers Hall to talk with Holly."

## Chapter 15

Towering over fifty stories, Bankers Hall is at the heart of a spider's web of pedestrian malls that connects thousands of shops and businesses to Prince's Island Park to the north (where last year there was a bona fide troll sighting, believe it or not) and to the Olympic Plaza and City Hall to the east. It is also home to Star Corp Petroleum, where serious players in the oil and financial worlds cut deals worth more money than I'll ever see in a thousand lifetimes.

Oh, and I should mention the distinctive crowns of both buildings are designed to look like *cowboy hats* when viewed from afar. Talk about tacky.

Betty, Marcus and I wandered through the mall until we reached the huge foyer of the east tower and sauntered up a corridor containing two sets of elevators. Sure, we probably stuck out like a sore thumb, particularly Betty's garish leopard skin outfit, but really, unless you're wearing an expensive business suit that costs more than a month's worth of groceries, you're going to get a lot of stares in a building like Bankers Hall. A pair of elevators arrived simultaneously, so we waited a moment and hopped on the one that had collected the fewest people. Within a minute or so, the large shining brass doors opened on the forty-sixth floor, and we casually walked into another foyer, this one with the Star Corp Petroleum logo embedded in the shining granite floor.

Marcus and Betty sat down on a pair of luxurious leather chairs as I shuffled up to a mahogany reception desk that was about as big as my bedroom. A very curt woman of about fifty with a wireless microphone hanging down from her ear raised a finger for me to wait as she finished directing a call.

"There," she said with a huff. "How can I help you?"

"I'm wondering if Holly Penske is in," I said, trying to sound about ten years older than I was.

The receptionist scanned me from head to foot and then arched a suspicious looking eyebrow. Her eyes panned across the foyer at Betty and Marcus sitting in silence, and then raised her other eyebrow.

"If you're looking for Star Corp to donate to your school, there's an application form and instructions on our website," she clucked.

"And that's *precisely* what I would have done had we been looking for a donation," I responded with a sweet smile on my face. "Holly Penske, please?"

The receptionist looked put out as she glanced down at a flat screen monitor. She clicked away at the keyboard for a second and then said, "She's just out of a board meeting, I'll call her office. And you are?"

"Julie Richardson," I said tersely. "She'll know who I am when you tell her."

She grunted and tapped an impatient finger on the polished desk. "Ms Penske, there's a Julie Richardson here to see you... Right. Fine then. I'll let her know."

She clattered away at the keyboard again like she was deliberately trying to avoid conveying the message she'd received and then said, "Just have a seat with your friends. Ms Penske will be on her way out here shortly to meet you."

"Thanks," I said. I turned on my heels and sauntered over to the plush leather chairs and considered for a moment that if and when we rescued my mom, she was going to rip me a new one because I'd sought out Holly Penske.

Betty was still scowling as I sat down on the chair between she and Marcus, and I'd given serious consideration that her face might possibly be frozen that way since she'd been scowling for the last thirty-five minutes.

"Who's Holly Penske?" asked Marcus.

"A very powerful entity in Prada shoes," I said. "She's in the know about all the supernatural goings-on around town. I thought to see if she could offer us a bit of help. Oh, and she's an immortal."

"Are you serious?"

I nodded. "Yep. Prepare to have blown your mind again."

Marcus shrugged. "Meh, I'm used to it. So, is she a good guy or a bad guy?"

"She's a troublemaker," Betty snipped. "That's all you really need to know."

"In what way?" he asked.

"In more ways than you can count. Julie, there is nothing she can offer you that either of you have the ability to pay for. We should leave."

I held up my hand to cut her off as I glanced down the long polished corridor to see a leggy woman with perfectly sculpted calves in a sharp navy blue skirt and matching blue blazer close a large office door and head toward us. Her midnight-black hair was cropped in a severe looking bob that contrasted with her flawless ivory skin and penetrating blue eyes. A group of men in business suits stopped chattering amongst themselves as the heels of her peep-toe pumps clicked loudly against the granite floor, almost demanding that everyone within earshot should immediately drop what they were doing and look at her. Her eyes fixed on me as she dropped a large manila envelope off to the evil receptionist from hell. She offered a warm smile and stuck out her hand as she strode across the Star Corp Petroleum logo to the waiting area.

"Julie Richardson and *company*," she said in a luxurious voice as her eyes darted over to Betty. "I see that my old acquaintance has found a new home. I do quite like the faux animal skin, Tutelary. Tell me; are you very much in demand these days?"

I could almost hear Betty's teeth grating together. "I'm where I'm needed," she said, icily.

"I'm really sorry to bother you, Holly," I said, standing up. "Something's happened to my mother. Something terrible."

"And you've come to seek my counsel," Holly said, her smile never wavering. "Well do follow me down to my office."

Holly's office was a huge room with black granite and marble pillars that stretched up more than twenty feet. The ceiling was of crystal clear glass and yet the room itself wasn't awash with sunlight. In one corner was a modern looking glass-topped desk and there was a very large, but very modest triangular table with leather cushions surrounding it at the centre of a sunken portion of the floor.

"Well, I'm never one to turn down a request for my counsel," she said, stepping down into the sunken floor and then taking a seat at the triangular table. "From the looks on your faces, I'd say that whatever has befallen your mother is rather… Shall we say, time-sensitive?"

I glanced at my watch as Marcus and I took a seat around the table. Betty chose to stand, her arms folded across her chest and her eyes fixed firmly on Holly. "That's right. I think we have less than two days to help her."

Holly nodded slowly as I relayed the events of the past two days. She walked over to the biggest wall unit of book-shelves I'd ever seen in my life, a look of deep concern on her face. She climbed a rolling ladder and pulled herself to a series of enormous volumes bound in bright red leather. "Here it is," she said with a look of satisfaction. She pulled a huge book off the shelf and rolled the ladder back to its original position. She heaved it under her arm and climbed down the ladder, while Marcus gave me a worried look.

"What's with the big honkin' encyclopaedia?" he whispered.

"It isn't an encyclopaedia, young man," she said as she dropped it on the table. It landed with a loud *slap*. "I am in no need of one."

"Then what's with all the books?" I asked.

"They're debt ledgers," Betty warned, "dating back a thousand years."

"Tack on another thousand years and you'd be correct, Tutelary," said Holly. "Julie, I'd be interested in learning what you might be able to offer me as a trade so that you won't become another signature among my records of those who owe me."

Of course I had nothing that Holly would want and she knew it, that's why she pulled out the book.

Fantastic.

Yeah, this was probably a dumb idea.

"I could let you borrow some of my magic," I said, immediately realizing how unbelievably amateur I sounded.

Holly let out a cold chuckle and shook her head. "Julie, respectfully, your magic is of no significance when compared to mine and you know it. But there are *other* things."

"You're not going to ask for my first born child or anything weird like that… Are you?"

Holly ignored my question and slid the book toward me. "I am counsel to seemingly insignificant practitioners like you, and large multi-national corporations like Star Corp Petroleum. The names of the directors of this company are listed alongside countless others who did not have an immediate way to compensate me for my insight."

Marcus piped up. "What if those who ask for your help aren't exactly working for the good guys?"

Holly's eyes shifted to Marcus. "There are no 'good guys' as you put it, boy. There are no bad guys either. Mortal concepts of right and wrong are unimportant to a daughter of the sun. However, profit is. Don't those of your kind deal in the sharing of information? How is my asking for compensation for a service that much different than a lawyer or an accountant asking to be compensated for their labours?"

Well, she had a point.

I placed my hand on the thick volume and it tingled at my touch. I hesitated a moment as I was about to open it and see what kinds of debts Holly had arranged for her debtors but she brushed my hand away at the last moment.

"That is not for you to see," she warned. "It would place a power imbalance in our *negotiations*."

"Is that what you're doing? Negotiating?" Betty snipped, her voice oozing with sarcasm. "I wonder what your contemporaries would say about forcing someone so young to be in your debt. It seems to me that more substantial deities living in the mortal realm would never take advantage of a mere child."

Holly glared at Betty so hard her eyes could have bored holes in the wall behind us. "Always the reasonable one, aren't you?" Her voice was flat and hard. "I am not in the business of providing free advice, not even to a child. I suspect others of my kind have made, shall we say, *alternative* arrangements."

"What kind of alternative arrangements?" I asked with a note of suspicion in my voice.

Holly pulled the book off the table and dropped it on the seat beside her. She folded her hands and her business-like demeanour returned. "I am aware of something from the spiritual realm that holds a great deal of malice towards witches. I am also aware there is a practitioner in the city acting as a vessel for this entity."

"I think I know who it is," I said. "Does the name Hudibras mean anything to you?"

She had a look of cold calculation in her eyes. "Before I answer your question it seems to me that alternate arrangement I mentioned should be discussed first."

"And what kind of alternate arrangements are we talking about, lady?" Marcus asked impatiently.

Holly's eyes narrowed as she opened a large drawer

in the table and pulled out a block of wood that was weathered with age. She flipped it over to reveal an engraving identical to the one I'd seen on the background of Hudibras' YouTube page.

"You're familiar with the person in this engraving, aren't you?" she asked.

"It's Matthew Hopkins, the Witchfinder General," I said, trying hard to conceal the uneasiness in my voice.

She nodded. "Very good. He is the entity I spoke of earlier. If I'm to offer you assistance, then I'd like you to capture his essence and return it to me."

I blinked hard. "I can't imagine why you'd want his spirit."

Holly relaxed a little and she folded her hands on the table. "I have my reasons."

I could almost hear the veins throbbing in Marcus' forehead and the look on his face told me we were in for one of his rare tirades.

"Look, lady," he snapped. "We don't know anything about Hudibras, Matthew Hopkins, or whoever this Witchfinder General dude is, but you're just as bad as leopard-skin girl over here. You both speak in riddles, and you both know more than you're letting on. Betty can't offer information unless the right question is asked, and you probably know enough to help Julie save her mother, but you won't tell her how to find this guy! Julie, screw it. Let's just get out of here, okay?"

I motioned for Marcus to calm down as I opened my backpack and took out my amulet. I laid it on the table in front of Holly and said, "It's pretty obvious that I'm going to do what you want if I have a hope of getting my mom back. I guess you'll probably need this as a down payment if you're going to be giving me any useful information. But first, you know about this amulet, don't you?"

"It's very lovely," said Holly. "Copper is an exceptionally strong conduit of magical energy. Tell me, Julie, are you in a coven or are you home-schooled?"

"Mom hates the political stuff in her coven," I said calmly. "So yeah, I'm home-schooled."

Holly examined the sigil in the center of the oval disk and said nothing for a moment. She dangled the amulet by its copper chain and held it out in front of me.

"Do you know what this engraving is?" she asked.

I grabbed the amulet and held it in my palm. "It's a combination of images. One is an inverted letter *d*, which represents the first letter in my mother's name. It's attached to the letter *j* for my first name. I've never been able to figure out why they're set in the middle of a serpentine shape."

Holly smiled warmly. "Really, that *is* interesting. Are you quite certain it's a serpentine shape because it *could* have a different meaning."

I gave her a confused look. "Excuse me?"

She stared hard at the amulet. "Tell me, Julie, do you remember anything of your father?" she asked.

I shrugged. "Just vague images from when I was very young. I have the occasional flash of a man with blond hair and bright eyes smiling at me. I mean, he died when I was four."

"And how did he die?" she asked.

"A car accident, why?"

Holly stood up from the leather cushion and returned to the book-shelves. She seemed to know exactly what she was looking for and this time she returned carrying another large volume with a dark green spine and gilded lettering.

"This," she said sliding the book across the table, "is a record of deaths among those in the local supernatural community. It goes back fifty years and you'll note that each entry contains an image of a tombstone or grave marking of some kind showing the last resting place of the departed. Tell me, do you often visit your father's grave?"

I gave her a confused look. "My father was cremated and his ashes were scattered from the highest point of Nose Hill Park. I was there. It's one of my earliest memories."

Holly remained impassive and pointed to the book. "Really. Are you quite certain of this?"

I pursed my lips and I flipped to the index and ran my finger down a lengthy list of alphabetized names until I found my father's. It said Stephen William Richardson was on page two hundred and four, so I searched through the book until I found the page with the entry for my father. When I saw the engraving of his grave marker, I gasped.

"The headstone has the same symbol as my amulet!"

"Indeed," said Holly, who looked very pleased with herself. "Odd that your father's headstone would have the same markings, isn't it? I wonder why your mother kept the location of your father's grave from you."

My head throbbed as I stared at the image of my father's headstone and I tried to force out any notion that my mother had been keeping a secret from me. So what if Stephen Richardson was also a witch? Witches marry one another all the time and the rite of pairing is one of the most important celebrations in all of witchcraft. But why hadn't she told me about his grave? I closed the book and gave it a hard shove back toward Holly.

"Stephen Richardson is long dead," I said coldly, as if to deflect Holly's insinuation. "It doesn't matter if my father was cremated or not, he can't help me and he can't help my mother."

Marcus put his hand on my shoulder. "You know, it's probably best that we leave, Julie. I'm sure Ms Penske has other deals to make with people who have more to offer than the spirit of the Witchfinder General. If we can somehow capture it."

Holly gave Marcus a sour look as she opened the book and flipped to the page with the engraving of my father's headstone. She slid it across the table toward me again and cocked a wary eyebrow at Marcus. "I admire your friend's protective nature, Julie, but he should know his place. Now, do have another look at that engraving."

I reached for the book and leaned over to see a faint etching of something written in Latin.

"*Servo parvulus,*" I said turning to Betty. "It means 'protect the child'. Is that a reference to *me?*"

She gave me an uncomfortable nod. I glanced back at Holly. She sat quietly with a satisfied smile and a large part of me wanted to reach across the table and slap it right off her face.

I glowered at her. "You, of course, know all about this secret information and you're more than happy to share if I have the ability to pay your fee, right?"

"I give this information freely," she said firmly. "But think about it. You possess a powerful focus for your magic at a point in time when all apprentice witches are still learning the basic functions of magic spells. You stood toe-to-toe with the blackest of magic before your mother showed up. And isn't it interesting that whatever dark force attacked you easily overcame your mother and yet somehow *you* succeeded in breaking the same spell your mother could not?"

Betty jumped to her feet. "That's enough!" she snarled, as she clenched her fists. "The girl is not yet prepared for what is to come. You will silence yourself *immediately!*"

The air crackled with magical energies as Holly glared at Betty. I could feel a steady hum of power growing in intensity and I noticed the room darken, as if the animosity between the two immortals was blotting out the unnatural light of Holly's office.

Holly's eyes glowed amid the gathering shadows. "The die is cast, Tutelary. She has been marked from birth and this is the first test she must complete. Her mother knew this. *You* knew this."

"She has not yet fully developed her powers," Betty said ominously. "She needs more time!"

I'd heard enough. I reached and drew a few wispy threads from the charged atmosphere inside the office until I could feel thousands of tiny electrical sparks coursing through my body. I pushed out my left hand and made a tight fist, and whispered, "*Hexus*". A glowing pillar of magical force dropped onto the center of the table like a sledgehammer, smashing it to pieces.

"I am in the room!" I shouted. "What's this rubbish about my not being prepared?"

Holly got up and circled the wreckage that had once been a table. "I won't charge you for damaging my property. I can only imagine the kind of stress you've been experiencing since your mother fell victim to Endless Night – such a despicable spell. Nevertheless, you would be wise to listen closely. Your kind has long feared that a new period of darkness would arrive wherein witches would once again face the hammer of persecution," she said ominously. "Of course, should this occur it will have no impact on immortals like your tutelary and me; but for a young practitioner like you, the future is potentially one of great peril."

I glanced at the amulet for a moment and then said, "You're suggesting there's some kind of organized movement whose sole purpose is to kill witches?"

"Not necessarily," said Betty. "There are always practitioners skilled in the dark arts whose agenda has more to do with acquiring a witch's power with the goal of strengthening their own abil–"

I cut her off. "Whoa! Wait a minute! If that person possesses a witch's soul, it would be like a supernatural battery that fuels their magic! If Hudibras is a vessel for Hopkins, then my mom's soul is just adding to his power!"

Betty looked at her watch and grimaced. "Speaking of batteries, this one is about to run dry. We have to leave soon so that Mrs Margaret Somerton's body can finish its journey. I'll have to find another one, it would seem."

Holly smiled and she motioned for us to follow her to the door. "I believe we have an arrangement, Julie. You'll bring me the spirit of Matthew Hopkins, won't you?"

I snorted. "Oh sure, no problem! I'll just kick his ass and trap his essence in another teddy bear. Easy-peasy!"

She opened the door and waved us through. "I knew you'd see it my way. I've provided you with a significant amount of information about your mother's predicament and a truthful – albeit disturbing – glimpse into your past. Finding and trapping the spirit of Matthew Hopkins is a small fee in the grand scheme of things."

"Don't mention it," I said sourly.

Holly reached into the breast pocket of her blazer and pulled out a small pad and pen. She jotted something down and then tore off the top sheet and handed it to me. "You'll need a bit of insight if you intend to find and trap Matthew Hopkins," she said.

I read the note and gasped. "Prince of Peace Cemetery plot eight hundred and forty-three, archival record number seventy-one. Is this the location of–"

Holly smiled politely and closed the door behind her.

"Your father's grave," she said. "I suspect you'll want to talk with him."

## Chapter 16

What had started as a poltergeist in the home of a little old lady had morphed into something beyond my ability to control. I was completely out of my league and no matter how hard I tried to push it away, self-doubt was starting to tear my belief in myself to shreds. I wracked my brain for some kind of quick solution, but there were none to be had – someone else was pulling the strings. Someone with a grudge against witches meant to single me out, to separate me from the one person who truly understood the dangers that were out there.

I stood in the foyer of Bankers Hall and stared hard at the note. Was my life up until now a lie? Why hadn't I been told about my fathers' final resting place? He died more than a decade ago and I knew so little about him that I sometimes wondered whether he ever existed at all. My father was a witch; that much I'd figured out during my meeting with Holly Penske. Mom told me she'd met my father at the farmer's market more than twenty years ago, and she said he was an honest but flawed man.

I'd come to know better than to press her on why she felt that way and over the years my father slowly faded from our conversations. In fact, I eventually decided to stop asking questions at around age eight because whenever I did, Mom would tense up like she was expecting to get a tetanus shot from the doctor. Her entire mood would change from 'earth-child free spirit' to 'dark and brooding creepy mom'. I took those mood swings as a clear indication that some things were better left unsaid, and my father disappeared – at least the memory of him did.

But now it was all coming back and it stabbed at my heart like an ice pick.

I remember being a very young girl, and my mother telling me that my father had gone to heaven. It didn't really register that he was never coming home until we scattered his ashes to the four winds on a brisk autumn afternoon and the grim faces on the cluster of fellow witches told me that something dark and terrible had happened. But why hadn't she told me about his grave? My head was spinning and I fought back a torrent of emotions as I buried my confusion and hurt deep down inside because despite all the secrets and revelations, being angry at Mom felt like I was somehow betraying her.

And she was all I had in this world. I needed her.

Betty was tapping one of her patent leather pumps

on the grass impatiently and I gave her a suspicious look.

"What?" she said, her voice taking on a sharp edge.

"You know way more than you've been letting on, Betty," I grumbled. "Is this the actual location of my father's remains?"

"It is," she said, half-nodding.

"And he's a ghost, is that it?"

"Somewhat."

I said nothing for a few seconds and then asked, "Did he really die in a car crash when I was four?"

Her eyes narrowed and she smoothed her skirt. "Yes, but it was no accident," she said flatly. "You know where to find him, young lady, so it's up to you at this point to decide whether you're ready to learn about your magical pedigree."

"*Pedigree?*" I gave her a frustrated glance. "This just keeps on getting better and better, doesn't it?"

Betty frowned. "Revelations are rarely pleasant, Julie."

Marcus grabbed my backpack and handed it to me. He'd said little since we left Holly's office and I could tell by the worried look in his eyes that he was afraid for my safety.

"Let's go home, Julie," he said softly. "Maybe the docs at the hospital will figure out how to help your mom."

"This is dark magic we're dealing with, Marcus," I said in a tired voice. "The clock is ticking and Holly said that my father could help us save Mom... we need him. *I* need him."

He heaved a sigh in resignation and then reluctantly nodded. "So we're hopping on a bus to the cemetery then?"

I tried to give him something resembling a hopeful smile because I knew Marcus felt a thousand percent useless and all he'd be able to offer would be moral support. I turned to Betty and pointed to her watch.

"How much longer do you have in Mrs Somerton's body?" I asked.

"Not long enough to accompany you to the cemetery. I need to find a new host as quickly as possible, so it's your decision as to what happens next."

I chewed my lip for a moment and glanced at my watch. The timer was counting down, we had to meet with my father's ghost and still find time to head to the Beltline and check out whoever Hudibras was. Clearly it was going to be a long night.

"Marcus and I will head to Prince of Peace Cemetery," I said, trying desperately to sound decisive. "You go do whatever is involved in finding another suitable host and meet us there."

Betty gave a reluctant shrug. "Very well. Do be careful, young lady."

We jumped on the Cambrian Heights bus and headed north. The trip took a little more than forty minutes and the sun was hanging low in the sky. It was shortly past 9.15pm when we hopped off the bus and headed up Fourth Street, the wrought-iron gates of the cemetery in view. I clutched my amulet tightly in my right hand as we passed the cemetery office, its neat pastel stucco and tidy flowerbeds offered a surreal contrast to the acres and acres of cold marble and granite headstones that rolled out like a carpet as far as the eye could see. Giant poplar trees on either side of thin, asphalt paths stood in elongated rows like soldiers on a parade ground and cast thick black shadows across the pavement. The main road meandered beyond a series of crypts that dated back to the early twentieth century and I recognized some of the names as being prominent Calgarians whose lineage carried on to the present day. Marcus quickened his pace in the gathering twilight and it was pretty clear he was nervous about being surrounded by the dead.

I couldn't blame him. Cemeteries are creepy places in broad daylight and they're the equivalent of a supernatural Costco when darkness sets in. The dead appear and disappear just as quickly as contestants on a reality TV show, and their presence hardly ever registers with most people in the mortal realm. If you're a witch, however, your senses are fine-tuned like a paranormal satellite dish and the dead surround you like hordes of last minute shoppers on Christmas Eve. So yeah, there were spectral figures poking their heads around gravestones and mausoleums but the only two living things in the cemetery were of little concern to them.

I wasn't about to tell Marcus about them.

I didn't know the layout of the cemetery so I wasn't exactly sure where my father's plot was located, despite the note from Holly. Not that it would have mattered much, because I could always ask someone for directions.

You know, someone who's been *dead* for decades.

I decided that since Marcus was probably feeling like he was of little help to me in my search, I'd throw him a bone.

"I don't know where to start looking," I grunted, as I stared at the note and hoped Marcus wouldn't realize I was lying through my teeth. "Under normal circumstances I'd go in the cemetery office and ask for directions, but it's past nine. Any ideas?"

He glanced at the now crumpled sheet of lined note paper and pointed to a three-foot tall wooden post at an intersection between two paths. "There's a sign up ahead. It says one-twenty to one-sixty. Your dad's plot is eight hundred and forty-three, so I think we need to stay on this main road. Oh, hey. If I'm a bit freaked out it's because ghosts shouldn't exist, so I'm just trying to get my head around all this."

I playfully nudged him in the ribs. "Maybe he'll haunt you."

He quirked an eyebrow and gave me an amused smile. "If he did, it'd be a chance to see if he emits any kind of radiation. He has to emit some kind of energy that you can measure."

"Nice," I said as I leaned into his shoulder. "In all seriousness, I haven't seen my father since I was a little kid. It's hard enough to reconnect with someone you haven't seen for years when they're alive, but a ghost? I'm so out of my element here it's not funny."

Marcus nodded as we continued up a hill littered with row upon row of military headstones. I spotted the spectre of a First World War soldier dressed in puttees, his tin helmet sitting at an angle over the near-translucent face of a young man. He couldn't have been much older than Marcus or me. He nodded politely and pointed to the highest spot on the hill.

Apparently someone was expecting us.

"Are you going to be okay?" Marcus asked quietly, his voice full of concern.

"I hope so," I said, matching his tone. "I haven't felt my father's presence since I was a little girl and part of me thinks this is really going to be like two strangers meeting for the first time. Anyway, it has to be done and you know what? I'll take the lingering spirit of my late father over not having him in my life any day of the week."

Marcus placed a hand on my shoulder and I stopped in my tracks. He turned to face me and said, "You rock, Julie. I just want you to know that."

I nodded and tried to smile, "Marcus, about what happened in the basement. When you said you thought I was beautiful. I didn't mean to–"

Just as I was about to apologize for stomping all over poor Marcus' heart the *Doctor Who* theme cut through the eerie silence of the cemetery.

"Shit," Marcus said, as he reached for his cell phone. "It's Marla. I told her I couldn't help her study tonight."

A wave of jealousy rushed through me as I snatched the phone out of Marcus' hand and read the text message.

*DarkChik: What r u doing? Want to hang out?*

I immediately gave Marcus a cold, hard stare and handed the cell phone back to him. "Marla wants to hang out? What is *that* about?"

"Christ!" he choked. "I don't know what the hell she's texting me for – she's *your* freaking girlfriend!"

"Well you must have given her your number, Marcus," I said in an accusatory tone. "Hey, if you'd rather hang out with Marla when I'm going through a crisis, don't let my shit stop you."

Marcus eyed flashed with anger. "Okay. First off, I texted her my cell number because I thought she needed help studying and I was in a charitable mood at the time. And second, when *haven't* I been there for you, Julie? You're my best friend! Third, even if I wanted to hang out with Marla, I'm allowed to do that. It's called being social. So instead of ripping me a new one, maybe you might want to consider the reason I'm here is because I actually give a rat's ass that my best friend's mother is in the hospital and there's some nasty ass bad guy out there who did it."

Well, that was a first. I'd never known Marcus to ever dress me or anyone down like that in his entire life, so clearly I'd touched a nerve. Did I mention that I'm an asshole with a capital A?

Marcus thumbed the keypad furiously and I said, "What are you telling her?"

"Well, it's not really your business what I tell anyone in a private conversation, Julie. But, in the interest of getting on with finding your dad's ghost, I'm texting her that I'm checking in on you and if Marla was really your friend, she'd be doing the same."

I immediately reached out and placed my left hand over the phone. "Hey, look, I'm sorry okay? I don't know what the hell is wrong with me."

He looked up from the cell phone and I noticed the angry look in his eyes was melting away. "It's cool. I know you're freaked out right now, but try to remember that I am too. And remember that I'm on your side, Julie. I've always been on your side."

I could feel my throat tighten, so I clenched my jaw tightly and pushed back the urge to start bawling because I needed to keep it together. Too much was at stake.

"I know, Marcus," I said quietly. "And I apologize."

He grunted as he slipped his cell phone back into his pocket. "Fair enough. Are we going to do the ghost hunter thing now? Because it's getting dark."

"Yeah, let's go," I said. I gripped my backpack tightly over my left shoulder and took a deep breath.

It was time to meet Stephen Richardson.

*Chapter 17*

The small wooden sign pointed to a series of graves on the crest of a hill with a view of downtown Calgary. The sun was a thin amber streak on the horizon and the sky was painted with a flat row of clouds in purple and pink hues as the heat of the day gave way to a mild breeze coming in from the west. I could hear the *tick-tick-tick* of the cemetery's sprinklers in the distance and I hoped they were on a timer because the last thing I wanted when seeing my father for the first time in more than a decade was to look like a wet dog.

Okay so I was a *little* freaked out about meeting him.

Marcus hummed quietly as we left the asphalt path and wandered between two rows of headstones that curved around a concrete fountain with a statue of an angel holding a trumpet as its centerpiece. The ghost of a woman wearing a flapper's dress with hair in a tight weave and a glittering headband pointed to the other end of the fountain and I felt a faint tingling of spectral energy brush against my face.

It felt mildly reminiscent of something I'd not felt in many years, and I knew we were close.

"Almost there," I whispered. "I can feel him."

"Is he going to be a poltergeist too?" Marcus asked nervously.

"Nope," a voice answered from behind us.

"Shit!" Marcus blurted. He stumbled over a flat grave marker and landed flat on his face. I spun around and drew on my magic, sending out a wave of compressed force that shot through the midsection of the spectre, blasting a small wrought iron bench and sending it careening ten feet into the air. It landed with a dull thump beside a large poplar tree.

"Nice way to say hello, pumpkin," the spectre said. "Good reflexes."

It was my father, and he looked just as I remembered.

You know, except that he was see-through.

He was stood about five feet away from me, his translucent arms folded calmly across his chest. He had a smooth complexion and a prominent nose that was framed by a pair of chubby cheeks. His hair was neatly cropped in a military style taper, and I could see that it was thinning along the top. He was dressed in a Spider-Man t-shirt along with a pair of Bermuda shorts and he was wearing sandals with what looked to be white gym socks. Apparently my father had no fashion sense, even in the afterlife.

Oh, and he was floating about six inches above the ground.

"Dad?" I said, in barely a whisper.

The ghost smiled faintly and nodded once. "Too many years have passed since I last saw you and by God, haven't you grown up into a beautiful young woman! You have your mother's eyes and you're as graceful as she looked on the night of our very first date – it was a night like tonight. You know, except we weren't in a cemetery – actually I first met your mom in a line at Peter's Drive-In during the summer solstice. Is it still in business? Best milkshakes in the Western Hemisphere, I swear."

"It's still there," I said.

He gave me a mournful look for half a second. "Man, what I wouldn't give for one of those shakes again. Anyway, I've been following you since I detected your magic when you got to the cemetery. You're going to want to work on your peripheral focus, kiddo. It'll save your bacon one day, trust me."

"But the ghost of the soldier pointed our way up here."

"To my grave," he said, as he floated over to Marcus who was slowly getting back to his feet. "Who's the skinny fella?"

"His name is Marcus," I said, hoping like hell that my best friend wouldn't faint in my father's presence.

"Marcus Guffman?" he said in a surprised voice. "Amanda and Wallace's kid?"

"Un-freaking-real!" Marcus said in astonishment. "I can see you plain as day! Man, I wish I had my spectrometer because up to now, Julie's been the one who can see ghosts, not me."

"Just means your mind is open enough to let you see the kinds of things most people turn a blind eye to, kid," he said.

"You *know* me?" Marcus asked.

"Knew you. Everything is past-tense when you're dead. Anyway, your mother met Julie's mom at daycare. We had your folks over for dinner a few times. They still alive?"

"Dad!" I said, shocked that even a ghost could manage to embarrass me in front of a friend. "That's totally *not* cool."

"Rats. Sorry, kiddo. That came out the wrong way. Here, sit with me for a moment. We need to have a little heart-to-heart and time is running short."

I walked over and sat down beside him. Marcus kept his distance but eyeballed my father closely. My head was filled with a stew of thoughts and intense feelings that I had no way of processing. Dad had been gone for so long, and now here he was sitting beside me. His vaporous body shifted and stirred with supernatural energy and I had to stop myself from reaching out to touch him out of fear that if his spiritual form were to come in contact with my magical energies, that he might disappear entirely.

"Dad," I said, as my throat tightened. "I want to stay with you here more than you can possibly imagine, but I need your help like I need air to breathe.

Mom is in the hospital. Something attacked my school and–"

"And you're hot on the trail of the culprit, sweetheart, I know. The spirit world's a big place and word travels fast among those of us who still hang out with the living. You going after whoever did this is pretty brave, kiddo. It's a helluva thing to duke it out with someone who can overpower a witch with your mother's experience and I'm proud of you for fighting back. I just wish I could be the guy fighting back; you're still so damned young."

"Thanks," I said. "How did you know I'd go after who did it?"

He appeared to take a deep breath and then he exhaled slowly. "Because that's what I would be doing, even if I were out-gunned. Then again, a Shadowcull is pretty much out-gunned every time he or she does the dirty work for the covens. Hell, I'd tag along with you, sweetheart, but I'm bound to this place until your mom joins me in the afterlife."

Marcus edged closer and appeared to be a bit more relaxed. "I should probably be bouncing off the walls right now because ghosts aren't supposed to be real and here we are in a creepy cemetery talking to one, but what the hell. Mr Richardson, what's a Shadowcull?"

He shrugged. "If the average, run-of-the-mill witch is responsible for protecting the world of mortals from the things that go bump in the night, then a Shadowcull is the one who prevents that bump in the night from happening in the first place. This city has been without a resident Shadowcull for more than ten years – until now."

I arched my eyebrows. "What do you mean by *until now*?"

He turned his wispy face toward me and gave me a worried look. "It's your birthright, sweetheart. My blood runs through your veins and that sets you apart from all the witches in your order. I'm going to throw caution to the wind here and ask you, why do you think your mom has disavowed her own coven?"

"Because she hates all that political stuff," I said. "At least that's what she's told me all my life."

He grunted. "Yeah, that's part of it. The other part is that they'd have seconded you to become a Shadowcull's initiate and you'd be trained up to mete out coven justice to anyone who posed a threat to the mortal world."

"Coven justice? But I thought that's what tribunals were for!"

"You're not entirely wrong, sweetheart. But a Shadowcull works outside the boundaries of what the average person would say is *ethical*. He or she is dispatched by a coven to use any and all means necessary to eliminate a threat up to and including the use of black magic."

I nearly fell off the concrete bench at my father's revelation. *Black magic?* It was black magic that was responsible for putting Mom in the hospital and I didn't want any part of it. "What if I have no interest in being a Shadowcull?" I said indignantly. "Don't I get to have a say?"

My father's look of concern wasn't going away. "It's your pedigree, Julie, and your magical signature makes you stand out like bonfire at midnight. You have to learn how to defend yourself against the Left Hand Path because they'll be coming after you, and sweetheart, those guys will stop at *nothing*."

Marcus adjusted his backpack and let out an exasperated sigh. "Here's what I'm not getting: if Julie is supposed to have some kind of special skill because her father was a so-called Shadowcull, well how can she be expected to do what you did in life when nobody has ever taught her? I mean, how can she protect herself?"

Dad let out an amused chuckle proving that ghosts, apparently, still have a sense of humour. His wispy form disappeared, reappearing less than a second later on his headstone about twenty feet away.

He pointed to a shovel at the foot of his grave and said, "How does she protect herself? She starts digging."

## Chapter 18

Marcus was knee-deep in soil as I kept a watchful eye for anyone who might see us. It was pitch black now thankfully, the quarter-moon concealed by clouds. The only sound that could be heard besides the sound of shovel-fulls of moist earth being dumped into a pile next to my father's headstone was the sound of Marcus cursing under his breath.

"Aside from being highly illegal, Julie," Marcus griped, "I'm not sure if digging up your Dad's grave while he looks on from the spirit world is either unbelievably creepy or points to the most dysfunctional family in human history. I'm *not* opening the casket!"

My father's form dissolved from the top of his headstone and reappeared beside Marcus. "There's no casket, kid," my father whispered. "If my body hadn't been cremated, one of my enemies would have dug me up and they'd have probably sold my corpse to a necromancer, and jeez, who wants that? Some of my ashes are mixed in with the soil and there's nothing of any

value in my grave unless you know what you're looking for. Just keep your eyes peeled for a copper box
because all the answers are in there. Trust me on this."

I hunched over as Marcus carefully pushed the
blade of the shovel down into the dirt. The edges of a
copper box became visible. He prised it out of the
ground with the shovel and dumped it at his feet. He
exhaled heavily and reached out to brush off chunky
clumps of moist clay.

"Wait a minute, kid," my father warned. "You
touch that thing and you're going to be in a world of
hurt."

Marcus glanced at my father through the corner of
his eye. "Protective spells again?"

"Yep," Dad's ghost made a grunting sound. "That
box is laced with sigils that I etched right into the metal.
Kiddo, I'm a member of the dearly departed, so I can't
disarm the spell. Looks like it falls to you."

I blinked a couple of times and held out my right
hand to feel through the layers of magic surrounding
the box. "It's a very complex protective ward," I said,
concentrating. "But it feels familiar somehow, like I've
seen this magic before."

My father's ghost nodded. "That's because I designed
it to be recognizable to only one person – you."

Marcus grabbed my wrist. "Be careful, Julie."

I let out a nervous sigh as I closed my eyes tightly.
Within seconds, my focus was immersed in multiple
layers of interlocking magical energies that had been

knitted together like a thick wool sweater. Strand after strand of emerald energy glowed in the darkness like individual lengths of neon, humming and throbbing as I carefully searched for a loose thread. After a moment, I'd found what I was looking for and I reached out with a whisper of magic, giving it the tiniest of tugs. The complicated protective ward surrounding the metal box slowly dissolved at my command and I gave another whisper of my magic for good measure.

"I-it's disarmed," I said quietly, as a bead of sweat rolled down between my shoulder blades. "I don't know how I did it, but it's disengaged."

"You drew on a deeper level of magic, kiddo," said my father with a twinge of pride in his voice.

I smiled at him for a short moment and then gazed down at the box. I slid a brass bolt on the front of the box. I took a deep breath to compose myself and then carefully lifted up the lid. The interior was remarkably dry; in fact it looked like the contents had been hermetically sealed from the elements. I shrugged and decided that my father's magical ward must have been stitched together so tightly that not even moisture from the ground would be able to penetrate the box. Inside were two items: a thick book with a drab olive cotton duck cover and a smaller wooden box with complex runes and sigils engraved in its smooth, rich surface. I reached for the book and pulled it out of the metal box.

"Your grimoire," I said with a bit of an edge in my voice. "Don't tell me, it's a Shadowcull's diary."

"Sort of," my father said. "My grimoire was always intended to be yours one day. It contains notes on the arcane, strategies and techniques to defeat dark agents; a who's-who of the magical world. All the main players are listed in that book, not to mention whether they are an ally or someone to be watched closely."

I unzipped my backpack and slipped both the box and the book inside. I reached for the wooden box and tried to open it but the tiny locking mechanism wouldn't budge.

"It won't open," I said, holding the box up for my father's ghost to see.

He nodded. "I know. Do you have your amulet? That's the only thing that will open it, and you'll understand why in a moment."

I reached into the hip pocket of my jeans and pulled out the amulet. I gave it a small rub with my thumb and then held it like a poker chip over the tiny locking mechanism. There was a quick snap as the metal bolt disengaged. I opened the box.

Inside was a two-inch wide copper band.

"It's a bracelet," I said, sounding slightly deflated. "It looks too big to fit me, Dad, and I already have my amulet to use as a focus for my magic."

"Uh-huh," he said in a knowing voice. "Put it on."

I took out the bracelet and examined it for a moment. It was highly polished and resembled the colour of a freshly minted penny. There were no sigils or engravings on its smooth surface but there was an oval recess about two or three millimetres deep in the center. It slid easily over my left hand and dangled loosely from my thin wrist.

"There's a hole in it," I said. "What's supposed to go in there?"

My father pointed to my amulet that was dangling from my fist. "It's a Shadowcull's weapon," he said. "The bracelet is a focus, just like your amulet, but when the two separate pieces are combined, it acts as an amplification device for magical energies. Slip your amulet into the recess and you'll see what I'm talking about."

I glanced at my amulet and then back to the oval recess in the bracelet. I shrugged my shoulders and unhooked the latch on the chain, then pulled the chain through the metal loop on the tiny charm. It popped into the recess with a click, and the band instantly tightened around my wrist. It was three sizes too big half a second ago and now it fitted snugly against my skin as if it had been custom-designed for me by a master craftsman. But that wasn't all. Not even close.

I felt an intense surge blast through my body as the bracelet's power intermingled with my magical signature. It was as if the bracelet had injected adrenaline into the naturally occurring magical forces from within and my spirit literally vibrated with magical energy. I took a hesitant breath as I glanced up at Marcus. He stood there with a blank expression but that wasn't what grabbed my attention: his entire face was encased in a blanket of colors ranging from Indian Ocean blue to deep sea Mediterranean green. His aura stood out like a beacon, swirling and crackling with living energy and I had to stop myself from reaching out to touch it, the colours were too vivid to be real.

I gazed out at my father and became speechless. Instead of the vaporous entity I'd spent the last hour with; his body had taken solid form as if he'd been coated with a shimmering film of light. I climbed out of the hole and gazed out in wonder at the cemetery. All around me were the spirits of the dead, all radiating different intensities of spectral waves as far as the eye could see.

And I could hear things.

The sound of a moth's wings beating with percussive rhythm like a helicopter blade slicing through the air. I shut out the sound of flying insects to hear dew forming on the grass beneath my feet. I looked down to see one tiny distinct droplet of moisture rolling down an individual blade of grass. I spun around as Marcus climbed out of the hole. I could hear his heart beating and the sound of his blood pulsing through his veins and I could even feel slightest variations in his body temperature.

"You will know your surroundings, Julie," my father's ghost whispered. "Your instincts will be heightened to such an extent that you won't need to think about what to do next when your enemies come for you. And they will come, sweetheart. They will come for you because you represent the clarity of magic's purpose and because you wield a power they covet. Their agents will try and turn you because to have a Shadowcull in their employ would be a prize worth killing for. They killed me because I let down my guard, so take my advice to heart. Never, ever take that bracelet off. Never lose that amulet and finally, never let your weapon fall into the enemy's hands."

"Anything else?" I asked as I ran my thumb along the smooth surface of the bracelet.

He nodded again. "Yeah, if the amulet has been fixed on the bracelet for more than a day, you need to remove it otherwise the amplifying effect will basically melt your brain and you'll go nuts."

"Seriously?"

"Dead serious," he said, stony faced.

I exhaled very slowly as my senses took in my surroundings. The shadows bent and flowed like liquid smoke as the clouds parted, bathing the cemetery in milky-blue moonlight. I could feel the vibration of traffic humming up and down Fourth Street beneath my feet and I heard the sound of a dog barking wildly in the distance.

I turned to my father who was floating like a fishing bob when I felt an electrifying jolt of dark energy set itself on the cemetery like a violent clap of thunder. An unearthly groan filled the air and both Marcus and I dropped to our knees and covered our ears to drown out the sound. It ended as quickly as it began and then

I felt the ground shake. All the colour drained from Marcus' face as he pointed to a copse of poplar trees less than a hundred yards from us.

"Holy shit!" he croaked. "Whatever the hell that thing is, it's huge and it's heading toward us!"

The air shook as the creature let out a roar that sent both Marcus and I tumbling into my father's grave.

"I know your name!" the creature shrieked, as it lumbered forward. In seconds it was on us.

## Chapter 19

I couldn't scream. It was as if the very sight of the monster sucked out the air from my lungs. Every muscle in my body was paralyzed with fear as the undead creature smashed through a granite crypt like a freight train. Marcus didn't waste any time and he instinctively grabbed my arm and hurled me from my father's grave with all his strength. Oh, and the copper bracelet decided all of a sudden to start glowing with a blinding white light. You know, because the twenty-foot tall creature comprised of body parts from nearby graves and bound together by the same spectral energy I'd felt at school actually *needed* help finding us. We tore across the crest of the hill until I spotted my father materialize beside a large crypt that resembled a gothic bungalow. He motioned for us to follow him just as the creature started running. Yeah, it *ran*.

"What the hell is that thing?" Marcus shouted as he dove headfirst into a finely manicured hedge surrounding the crypt. I hurdled over the hedge and landed badly, twisting my ankle.

"It's the same magic that was behind the attack at school!" I said, wincing from the pain.

"But it's a zombie!" he choked.

My father's ghost poked his head above the hedge and said, "It's not a zombie, it's about fifty yards away from here and you both are going to be deader than me if you can't think of something to stop it!"

Marcus turned his eyes toward me. "What are you going to do?"

"I have no idea," I said in a terrified voice. "I'm only trained in defensive magic."

"Yeah, well start thinking offensive!" Dad said in a determined voice. "It's twenty-five yards from here and it looks hungry. You're going to have to confront that walking morgue, and if it were me, I'd be using emotional magic!"

"My emotions?"

"All of them! You need to reach down into the very pit of your soul and channel your emotions into a spell that acts like dark magic. Remember, the bracelet will amplify your power, so it's up to you now! Go kick some ass!"

My heart was beating so fast I could feel the blood surging through my veins. I didn't want to stand up to that thing, but my father was right, we were dead if I didn't do something. I felt the copper band tingling with energy against my wrist and I took a deep breath.

I clenched my jaw and reached out with my spirit to the elemental forces that surrounded me. As if it were in tune with my supernatural instincts, the copper band exploded with spectral energy and blazed like a fireball as I built my focus into a brick wall of concentration. I fixed my eyes on a cluster of large granite headstones in front of the monster and roared, "*Ballisticus!*"

A tremor shook the earth as the headstones tore out of the ground and sailed through the air at the creature, pummelling it like an artillery target and sending it tumbling. It crash-landed against the cement fountain we'd been sitting on moments earlier. I pushed myself out of the hedge, my body vibrating with power, and stalked through the cool damp grass and onto an asphalt path.

"I'm not going down without a fight!" I barked, my body shaking. "I don't know what your beef is with me, but I'll torch this entire cemetery unless you give me back my mother!"

The creature slowly got back to its feet. Its face was a hideous mask of the features of three or four corpses stitched together with magic. Each face writhed; it was as if they were communicating a strategy to take me down. Four sets of hideous lips in various stages of decay curled up into four separate rotting grins as its eyes fixed on me. The left side of the creature's body sported three arms; two male and one female. There was one perfectly sculpted arm on the right side and each arm sprouted from four distinct torsos, compressed together, that looked like they'd been ripped from their former owners. The tight, grey skin of the rotting husks that made up the creature's body was visible through the torn remnants of burial clothes.

The creature opened all four mouths and let out a high-pitched wail that blasted through the air, sending me stumbling backward against the hedge. I scrambled to my feet and the creature rushed at me, a head-on collision waiting to happen. I held out my left arm and dug my feet into the ground as I summoned another burst of magic, this time calling up a pillar of force and blasting it straight into the center of the creature's mass. There was a loud splattering sound, and a rolling wave of vomit frothed its way up to my throat as I watched two of the arms and one torso ripped from the amalgam of decaying flesh. The faces looked surprised by my attack for half a second, and then they seemed to be communicating with each other again.

"Emotional magic, Julie!" my father's ghost bellowed. "You're not reaching deep enough!"

"I'm doing the best that I can!" I shouted.

"Do better!" he shot back. "You're a Shadowcull and you haven't even scratched the surface of what you're capable of!"

I gave my head a shake as I felt the ground tremble beneath my feet. Huge jets of earth and stone belched out from a dozen separate graves, toppling the headstones like they were dominoes. I gazed up, and what I saw next sent my heart racing.

Suspended high in the air like rotting marionettes were twelve corpses. Their burial garb was matted with smears of dirt and fluttered about as a cold wind kicked up dust devils beneath their dangling feet. Each pivoted toward me and then slowly floated to the ground. My mouth was bone dry and I tried to gulp but my throat was like sandpaper. Ice cold malice filled the air like a poisonous fog. I felt a tinge of something faintly familiar, and *very* focused on its task.

The creature dropped down onto the grass. There was a flash of photo-negative energy and the creature's body parts exploded apart in a blast of eerie green light. I was just about to exhale in relief when I saw twelve ribbons of spectral energy weave across the cemetery toward the rotting husks.

"Oh my God!" I whispered. Another jolt of panic shot through me. Each of the twelve corpses stretched out their arms. Their jaws opened wide and their hollow eyes rolled over to my position in front of the hedge. Slowly, deliberately, they began to stagger forward.

"Run!" I shrieked. I leaped over the hedge, completely forgetting about the pain in my ankle.

The creatures lumbered on, their lifeless eyes staring straight ahead and yet they somehow managed to keep in a line. The copper bracelet stung like sunburn against my skin and I grunted through my teeth as I leaped over another hedge, Marcus in tow.

"You can't outrun them, Julie!" my father shouted as he floated backwards about thirty feet in front of us.

"This is dark magic we're dealing with and those things are going to keep coming after you, even if you make it back home!"

I came to a sudden stop. How in the hell was I supposed to take down a dozen revenants? My only exposure to the living dead had been through movies and TV, and now my father was telling me that I'd have to somehow come up with a spell to destroy them without getting our heads ripped off.

"They're latched onto my magical signature," I barked. "And that means someone is controlling them."

Marcus squatted and rested his arms on his knees. "So this is just another spell?"

"You bet it is," I said, as I stretched out my hands to see if I could triangulate the spell's source. "But where there's a spell there's always a path of flow for magical energy. It's pointless to duke it out because the spell will just spawn more of them."

"And there's probably a few thousand graves in this cemetery," my father said. "If it were me, Julie, I'd take an overhead view and see if you can tap into its location."

My jaw dropped at my father's suggestion.

Contrary to popular belief, witches don't hop onto the backs of their corn brooms and take to the skies. That said, science doesn't *always* apply to magic and because of this, witches have been known to *defy* gravity when the need arises. In short, we don't fly; we float.

Two simple words make up the *Volatilis* spell, but magic words and phrases, like my amulet and now my copper bracelet, are merely a focus that allows magic to flow through a practitioner. A spell like the *Volatilis* is something only a seasoned practitioner can actually pull off and, like all magic, it takes intense concentration and the practitioner runs the risk of crash-landing if they're fatigued. I was already feeling the throbbing pain of a twisted ankle and the blast I'd sent at the creature had weakened me. To make matters worse, I'd never before attempted the *Volatilis* and I knew of no witch who could do it.

The extended line of undead creatures plodded along, tripping over headstones and clumsily getting back to their feet. They were about two hundred yards from us. I gave my father a pained glance. "You can do it, Julie," he said with an air of authority. It was almost as if he knew what was going to happen next.

I took a deep breath and grabbed Marcus by the scruff of the neck. "Put your arms around me."

"Um, sure?" he said in a nervous voice as he wrapped his bony arms around my midsection.

"Close your eyes and don't ask questions," I said as I tried to ignore the fact that this was the first time any boy had put his arms around me and that it was actually kind of hot. "Just *trust* me, okay?"

I squeezed my eyes tight and reached for my magic. The copper band hummed as I shut out the sounds of the night and dug down as deep as I possibly could. It was time.

I lashed out in a voice that blasted through the air. "*Volatilis Levitata! Volatilis Levitata! Volatilis Levitata! Volatilus Levitata! Volatilis Levitata!*"

I opened my eyes to see a whirlpool of magical energy above my head. Thin tendrils of magic reached over my shoulders and down to my feet like strands of spun gold, and I had to stop myself from reaching out to touch them. I pulled Marcus close to me and I tried to stifle my utter shock that the spell seemed to be taking hold. My feet were slowly lifting off the ground and I grated my teeth together as Marcus' weight threatened to short circuit the *Volatilis*. I pushed my focus deeper, drawing on all the supernatural energy in the graveyard to fuel the spell. It worked; we floated higher and higher into the air.

Marcus buried his head into the nape of my neck. That was actually kind of hot too, well, except for the fact that he was shrieking into my shoulder. I glanced at the copper band and had to turn away from its blinding white glow. It amplified my magic, pulsing with the power of the spell that carried us higher and higher.

"This cannot be happening!" Marcus wailed. "Human beings cannot defy gravity! No way this is real!"

The spell's magic poured through the supercharged atmosphere and into my body as I pushed forward, floating through the air like a human balloon as I looked for a safe place to deposit Marcus. "It's happening! I don't know how I did it, but it's really happening!"

"Good luck to Stephen Hawking if he tries to figure

this one out!" he whispered in amazement. "Just don't drop me, okay?"

"Not a chance. I've got to get you to a safe place."

I looked around for my father and spotted him hovering beside an enormous poplar tree. The creatures were well behind us as I ducked into the dense foliage and deposited Marcus safely on a branch that looked like it was thick enough to support an elephant. I decided that it was time to use my peripheral focus to see if I could detect the path of flow for the dark spell that Hudibras was using to animate the corpses. The air was prickling with supernatural force, raising every hair on my body. I shut my eyes tight to allow my spirit to feel the waves of magic drifting through the cemetery.

I reached out through the complex tendrils of energy, sending my senses rocketing out of the cemetery, soaring over buildings and rooftops at blinding speed. Below me, entire neighbourhoods appeared and disappeared as my focus stormed past familiar city landmarks in the blink of an eye. I whizzed along sidewalks, dodging pedestrians and parking meters and cars at busy intersections. I barrelled skyward, over treetops and lampposts at breakneck speed until I spotted a sign that read 'Welcome to The Beltline'. Less than a second later my focus was hovering over a row of high-priced apartment buildings so I scanned the pebbled surfaces of each rooftop, ignoring the ventilation ducts and elevator shafts until I spotted it: the Baphomet Sigil.

The air carried the taint of malice and I could taste the bitterness of Hudibras' dark spell, but he was nowhere to be found. Suddenly I felt myself slingshot at near-warp speed through a magical wormhole until my mind realized it was back in the cemetery. I concentrated, letting the energy flow through me as I shaped my peripheral focus into an enormous magnet for dark magic. I grated my teeth together and pushed my new-found magical Sight to its breaking point, reaching out further and further across the rows of graves until I found what I was looking for.

I opened my eyes and gasped.

Below me as far as the eye could see was a tightly woven blanket of energies that pulsed and hummed in the darkness. Miniscule threads of purple light intermingled with thick strands of blues and greys that resembled the vapour trail of a jet plane. Plumes of ghostly mist shimmered and stirred like a bubbling stew, enveloping smaller, less dense clouds of energy, blending and swirling together as if they were all in an enormous pot.

I held out my left hand – my copper-banded hand, the hand of a *Shadowcull* – and clenched my jaw as I latched onto a trace of the malice. My body pivoted in the air, as if I were a needle on a compass, directing me to the source. Within seconds, I spotted it. Like a giant shining worm slithering across the pavement after a thunderstorm, the dark spell's path twisted through the maze of spectral energy. Even at one hundred feet in the air, I could taste its hatred.

It felt ancient, something that had been rotting beneath deep layers of dust and time. I could smell the faintest traces of burning coal and I could hear distant bloodcurdling screams. Terrified women's voices begged and pleaded as a chorus of self-righteous sounding males quoted biblical scripture. They spoke an older form of English, caustic and bitter, heavy with an accent that hadn't been heard in hundreds of years.

My mind flooded with images of damp stone walls and loose hay scattered across a plank floor. I could hear the hissing and crackling of fire and my nostrils filled with the smell of smoke and blood. I saw chains dangling from a wall and the image of an emaciated woman, old and bent double like a labourer who'd worked a lifetime in a stone quarry. The oil and smeared soot on her wrinkled face did little to hide the bruises and cuts around her eyes and mouth. Another image flashed, the old woman now lay stretched across an enormous tree trunk and her wrists were bound to her feet. Kneeling in front of her was a thin man with an almost regal bearing. He was clad in a doublet, a red velvet jerkin and hose that stretched up from his buckled shoes over his knees. A thick cloak was draped over his narrow shoulders and his cold, accusing eyes bore into the old woman like a pair of blades, cutting through her cries of pain like a butcher hacking through flesh and bone. I fought back bile because I'd latched onto a simmering hatred so bitter that it seemed to poison each breath I drew into my lungs.

"That's Matthew Hopkins," I whispered. "The Witchfinder General!"

I should have been terrified at my glimpse into the past, but fear was the last thing on my mind. That poor old woman was either a witch or someone who was falsely accused and there was nothing I could do for her since the image was just a shadow in time. Not that it mattered much because Matthew Hopkins was back with stone cold vengeance aimed squarely at me.

And I wasn't going down without a fight.

I drew my spirit into a counter-spell that would act like a computer virus, latching onto the menacing path of flow, short circuiting his magic and sending him a reminder that I was onto him. Black magic might be forbidden, but I was a Shadowcull and the vile image of inquisition and torture ignited a primitive set of emotions in me. Here was the entity that was responsible for what happened to my mother. He was close. So close I could push through his centuries of hatred and repugnance. So close I could almost reach out and tear the skin from his face. I was a Shadowcull. I had the ability and license to draw upon the darkest magic in the name of protecting the innocent and dispensing with anyone who would threaten me and those I loved. I decided then and there to lace my power with malevolence so that Hudibras would know that I wasn't going to go down without a fight.

The spell flew out of me as a toxic mixture of hatred, vengeance and rage. The words poured out of my mouth like a torrent of water through a spillway. My magic cascaded out, levelling headstones and hedges as a plume of brown dust and debris spewed high into the air. An inky column of black magic connected with Hudibras' spell like a battle tank smashing through a brick wall. A hundred feet below me, the rotting husks of the dozen creatures cried out in one shrill terrified scream, splitting the air with an explosion of pain and frustration. They dropped to the ground, writhing in agony as the magic that fuelled their decaying bodies shrivelled and withered like vines dying in a drought. I reached out, channelling my rage through Hudibras' spell, shaping and moulding it into a dagger that would mark my target. He was my prey now.

I watched with calm fascination as the energy of his dark spell dissolved like a morning fog burning off in the sunlight. I willed the *Volatilis* to carry me back to the ground and the last thing I saw as I drifted over the tree-tops was a scorch mark etched into the soft turf below.

It was my sigil, my mark and my birthright. I was a Shadowcull and it was payback time.

## Chapter 20

My father escorted us down a winding path leading to the north gate of the cemetery. Marcus said very little after witnessing me dispatch Hudibras' spell using dark magic.

You know, really nasty dark magic that was laced with every ounce of malice I could muster.

Yeah, he was pretty freaked out. Being chased by a swarm of rotting corpses bent on tearing your limbs off is probably a one-way ticket to the land of post-traumatic stress disorder, and my gut told me (not to mention the distance Marcus was now putting between himself and me) that he was probably scared to death of me now.

"You've no need to feel like you've broken a vow, kiddo," my father's ghost said. "Were you not a Shadowcull, yeah, your coven would be coming after you right now. Pfft, the idiots would probably try to plug you into some kind of deprogramming regimen."

I shrugged hard as we shuffled down a twisting

path. "I don't feel bad about it. I did what I had to do. I've marked Hudibras with my magic and now all I have to do is follow the trail right to him."

My father floated in front of me, as if to block my way down the path. His eyes narrowed and a look of foreboding washed over his face. "Yeah, well don't get too over-confident there, kiddo," he said grimly. "The spirit of Matthew Hopkins has spent more than four hundred years in the afterlife, bags of time to brood and plot against our kind. You need to understand that this guy was a pro during life. He used any and all means to extract a confession of witchcraft from thousands of innocent women and children. Don't even think for a moment that he doesn't have an arsenal of tools at his disposal to take you down."

"But spirits can't do magic, unless…"

"Unless they can latch onto someone who can," he said, finishing my sentence. "If their malice is strong enough, they can possess a human being just as well as a demon. I'd say your Hudibras is likely possessed, sure would explain everything that's been happening around town."

I dug my index finger underneath the copper bracelet and scratched. My wrist and forearm had been itchy for the past ten minutes and I made a mental note to carry some lotion in my backpack from now on. I glanced at Marcus who was still four or five paces ahead of us. His hands were dug into his pockets and his backpack dangled limply from one hunched shoulder as he followed the path around a cenotaph, its small flame flickering away in the darkness. I could see the wrought iron gates of the cemetery ahead and I knew my visit with my father was nearly over. It wasn't the kind of homecoming I'd have liked, but then again, I'd only known that his spirit still lingered in the world of the living for a few hours.

There was so much I wanted to ask him about Mom and our lives together before he was taken from us and there were still those faint wisps of memory of my living father: a strong warm hand brushing against my left cheek when I had chickenpox; the sensation of being lifted high onto his broad shoulders and seeing the world though his grown up eyes. I wanted to rekindle the feeling of being scooped up in his arms as I ran to him after being frightened by a hippo at the Calgary Zoo. Most important, though, I wanted to know who was responsible for the car crash that claimed his life.

"We don't have a lot of time left tonight," I said, slowing down my pace. "You told me that you dropped your guard and that's why you were taken from Mom and me. Do you have any idea who was responsible?"

My father floated down to eye level and he clenched his jaw. "That's a good question, kiddo," he said in a dark voice. "And one that can be answered another time. You go get your mom back. You've got more pressing matters for now."

"It matters to me," I said flatly.

Dad offered a regretful shrug and glanced at Marcus

and then back at me. "I don't have a clue who took me down, sweetheart. When this is all over, you and me, we'll work together to find whoever did it, okay?"

I nodded. "What I'm not getting is why Mom hasn't come to visit you. I mean… Maybe it's just me, but that seems to be something regular people do."

"Practitioners aren't regular people, sweetie," he said calmly. "Anyway, who says that she hasn't?"

"What?" I nearly shrieked. Marcus turned around and offered a concerned look that did absolutely nothing to buffer the shock of the news that my mother had been coming to the cemetery to visit my father without telling me.

"It's really complicated, sweetheart," Dad whispered. "I know what it looks like and your mom is innocent of all charges, got it? She wanted to bring you here ever since you were a little girl and I talked her out of it."

"But why?" I asked in confusion. "What on earth for?"

"To protect you," my father said firmly. "I didn't want my enemies to know that your magical signature came even close to resembling mine until you were strong enough to hold your own, plain and simple. Your mom argued like a crazy woman that you should be allowed to visit me and I absolutely refused. The risk was too great."

It was everything I could do to keep myself from having a meltdown right then and there in the middle of the cemetery. All those years without him might not have happened if Mom had shared the knowledge that his spirit lingered on in the world of the living. I knew that everything he was saying about the risk was probably right, but it did little to soften the pain at knowing that he wasn't gone. Surely there could have been some way for me to have visited with him that didn't put me at risk? Surely his enemies knew that person visiting his grave was his wife and the mother of his child?

Marcus seemed to shrink a little. "Julie, your dad is right. They had to protect you. *Servo Parvulus*, remember?"

I ground my fists into my eyes in an attempt to stop myself from bawling. "I know it was the right thing to do, but it feels so wrong," I whimpered and turned to face my father. "Someone killed you, Mom's going to probably die and I'm the next one on the hit list. Look, Dad, I understand that you both had to protect me, but damn, if she could have at least told me you weren't gone forever; if she'd only let me know that you were here, somehow there could have been a way for me to see you."

"There was no possible way that could have protected you, sweetheart," my father said in a firm but tender voice. "Listen, sometimes fate forces you to grow up pretty darned fast, and this would be one of those times. It was my decision. You were too precious to be put in harm's way until you were truly ready."

I breathed out very slowly in an attempt to regain my

composure. There was no point in arguing about the past. It was pretty clear that if I could find Hudibras then I would find Matthew Hopkins. And once I'd found Matthew Hopkins I could extract his soul for Holly. My debt would be paid and I'd save my mom.

"And you really think I'm ready?" I asked with a sniffle.

"After what I've seen you do tonight, I think you're well on your way, baby girl," he said proudly.

I bit my lip and said, "All right, what's done is done. Any ideas on how I'm supposed to take down Hudibras, not to mention trap the spirit of Matthew Hopkins?"

My father let out a small dry cough and then said something so glaringly obvious that I felt like a fool for asking.

"Kiddo, you call him out and throw down."

## Chapter 21

As Marcus and I left the cemetery, I couldn't help but wonder where the heck Betty Priddy had disappeared to. She was supposed to be my guardian and while I could understand that she had to find another host since the body of Margaret Somerton had reached its best before date, it would have been nice if she'd given me a heads-up about a few things.

Like Shadowculls and coven justice, for example. No, wait. Betty couldn't volunteer information and would only give me answers if I asked the right questions; a lovely arrangement.

Marcus and I walked along the edge of the iron fence surrounding the cemetery. We said very little to each other as we headed to the Cambrian Heights bus terminal.

"It's ten to eleven," Marcus said quietly as he sent a text message to his parents. "I'm going to get hammered by my folks for being out this late on a school night, so I told them I'm crashing at your place. I hope they buy it."

"Sorry, Marcus," I said, sliding my hand around his bone-thin arm. "I've dragged you into all of this, just like I do every time, and I never take into consideration how hard it must be for you to be my friend."

He slipped his cell phone into his jeans and put his arm around me. "It's never been hard to be your friend, Julie. Anyway, I don't know how useful a friend I can be, what with all this supernatural crap flying at you from every direction. I guess the next thing on the to-do list is for both of us to head over to the Beltline."

I shook my head. "No need. I checked it out while you were hanging onto that poplar tree for dear life."

Marcus threw me a surprised look. "Come again?"

I waved my band covered wrist in Marcus' face. "Enhancing my magic isn't all this thing can do. Apparently when I'm wearing it, I can use my peripheral focus to do long range reconnaissance."

"No way!" he gasped. "So your mind left your body?"

I shrugged. As I spotted the 24-hour McDonald's across the road from the bus terminal, my stomach gurgled loud enough for both of us to hear. "I don't know how to describe it. What I can tell you is I saw what had to be a five-foot in diameter Baphomet Sigil on top of a ritzy looking apartment building. There was no sign of anyone there... Hey, are you hungry? We should get something to eat and formulate a plan, got any money?"

He smiled. "So let me get this straight: we nearly get killed by a bunch of zombies after digging up the grave of *your* father and *I* have to pay for the Big Macs?

Wait... I already know the answer, so yeah, I've got twenty bucks on me."

We consumed the Big Macs in less than two minutes. My hunger was temporarily sated, so I sat quietly and sipped away at my Coke as Marcus inhaled his French fries.

"You know," he said dipping a French fry into a tiny cup filled with ketchup, "Everything that's happened so far has been according to someone else's plan. One thing that doesn't make sense is the poltergeist at Mrs Gilbert's – the spirit of John Stearne."

"What about him?"

"Well, I don't see how he's connected to all this unless..."

"Unless what?"

He reached into his pocket and pulled out his iPhone. He slid his index finger across the touchscreen a few times and within seconds his face lit up like a Christmas tree.

"I freaking knew it!" he almost shouted. "I just Googled John Stearne and it turns out he worked with Hopkins back in the 1600s. Look!"

Marcus handed me his iPhone and I squinted to read a Wikipedia entry.

"'John Stearne was an associate of Matthew Hopkins the Witchfinder General,'" I read aloud. "'He was known at various times as the witch–hunter, and witch pricker John Stearne. A family man and land owner, he was ten years older than Hopkins. He maintained a house in Manningtree which is where he met Hopkins following Stearne's accusations against witches. Within a year of the death of Matthew Hopkins, Stearne retired to his farm and wrote A Confirmation and Discovery of Witchcraft.' Oh my God!"

"Oh my God is right," Marcus gasped. "Julie, this is huge!"

I nodded without taking my eyes off the tiny screen. "I know, but Stearne said that he'd been dragged back into the world of the living."

"Maybe Hudibras did it," Marcus said grimly.

"Maybe," I said as I stole one of Marcus' fries. "But I didn't detect any malice associated with Stearne's spirit. There wasn't a hint of it when the door blew in on the shed and the first time I felt malice bordering on full blown hatred was when I was attacked at school. I mean, I've been thinking about it and you know what? Hudibras has to be someone with a magical pedigree that packs a punch. There's just no way a malevolent spirit can do magic on its own; it simply can't be done."

Marcus grunted. "It seems like a heck of a lot of work to put together a YouTube video as a lure to smoke out a witch. That just doesn't add up somehow."

I blinked. "What are you getting at, Marcus?"

He pulled a notepad out of his backpack and cleared the top of our small table. With a click of his pen, he started writing and in less than a minute, he spun the pad around for me to examine.

"The attack on Mrs Gilbert was the first thing that happened. After that was the shed. Then we looked online for any weird poltergeist activity in town and that led to the YouTube video with those poor dogs. The next thing we did was to send an email and the very next day, the attack at the school happened. Call me crazy, Julie, but I'm not seeing any randomness with this at all. Everything points to someone who knows you – someone who knows how your mind works."

"How?"

Marcus stuffed the pen in a small pouch on his backpack and pulled the zipper. "Think about it, Julie. Someone had to know that you'd respond to the poltergeist at Mrs Gilbert's. They had to know that you'd go to your mom and exorcise the spirit. They'd have known that you'd use a tracking spell to find them and I'm absolutely certain they'd know that you'd look online for clues. It's just not random at all."

I stared at the list and was quiet for a moment. Marcus' hypothesis seemed plausible and I crunched my brain to figure out who might know me well enough to understand how my mind works, but to no avail. I could think of no one who would be a threat to me.

"I got nothing," I said, sounding deflated. "Mom's been out of the coven for years and the only people I can think of who understand how I'm hard-wired are Betty, Holly Penske, my father's ghost and you."

Marcus pointed a bony finger at my back pack. "That book of your dad's. Maybe it's got a spell you can use to take down Hudibras."

Well, it *was* a Shadowcull's grimoire. Surely there'd be something inside I could use to devise a plan for throwing down with Hudibras before the clock ran out on my mom. I unzipped my backpack and pulled out the two-inch-thick book. Marcus got up and dumped his tray of garbage as I started flipping through the yellow sheets filled with hand-written entries in a strange code that resembled Egyptian hieroglyphs.

It was an impressive work. There was no table of contents, only a page with a series of symbols and rubbings. I recognized the sigil from my amulet and decided that if the amulet could be used to unlock the box in my father's grave, it could also be used to decode my father's grimoire. I pulled my amulet off the thin copper chain around my neck and pressed it against the drawing of the matching sigil. Amazingly, the complex pattern of coded entries transformed into English and within seconds, I'd found an index.

"There's a section on something called 'quick spells'," I said as I searched for the right page. "I wonder what that's about."

Marcus leaned over so that his forehead was less than an inch from mine and I got that stupid little fluttering feeling in the pit of my stomach that told me that despite all the drama of the past few hours, my feelings for Marcus had grown stronger. I don't know if it was because we'd been nearly killed or the fact that we'd been riding an emotional rollercoaster together ever since the attack at the school, but Marcus stood by me. Even when I was being jealous and a general bitch, he didn't abandon me when any normal guy would have run for his life.

"What's it say?" Marcus asked.

I ran my finger along the middle of the page until I found something that looked like a definition. "'Quick Spells: For use when in the throes of a duel'. That sounds about right seeing as how I'm going to be going at it with someone who probably knows how to do magic on the fly. There's binding and summoning spells of every bloody description!"

"What's a binding?"

"It's a spell that's used to prevent someone from doing harm to another person."

"Gotcha. Well, there's a whack of bad ass stuff you can use," said Marcus pointing his pen at the last one on the list. "What's a black curse?"

I closed my father's grimoire with a loud slap. "You *don't* want to go there... seriously."

"What are you talking about?"

I felt a twinge of fear tie itself into a tight knot. "It's the last resort for black magic," I said sounding like the voice of doom. "It's the sorcery equivalent of mutually assured destruction."

Marcus gasped. "You mean like what they do with nuclear weapons? Like if you're going to go down you're taking every last one of them with you?"

I nodded slowly. "Yeah, that's pretty much it."

Marcus reached for the grimoire and I pulled it

away at the last second. "No… just *trust* me on this, okay? That's a completely taboo spell."

"Well, what's it do?" he asked.

I shuddered for a moment and clenched my jaw tightly. "A black curse sucks the life out of every single living thing within a hundred-yard radius, creating a black hole of negative energy from which it is utterly impossible for the intended victim to escape. Not only does it kill you, it erases you."

Marcus' eyes bugged out. "Cosmic obliteration," he said in a near whisper. "But… how is that possible?"

"A black curse draws on all the forces of the physical and spiritual worlds," I said slowly. "Meaning there would be no afterlife at all. No heaven or hell as a reward or punishment for deeds in life, just a vast expanse of non-existence. As if the very thought of you never happened and everything you touched during your life, everyone who ever knew and loved you would have never felt your presence. You would become *unborn*."

It was Marcus' turn to shudder. "You know, that's frankly a terrifying thought. It throws everything we know about physics and time right out the window."

"No shit," I said, glancing at my watch. It blinked 11:48pm. "We need to put a plan together super fast. Time's running out for my mom and if we're going to take down Hudibras, it's going to have to be done before sunrise."

"How come?" asked Marcus.

"Because there's going to be magic flying in every

direction and don't forget that we're dealing with a guy who likes to imitate the power of a poltergeist. Everything that isn't nailed down will be transformed into deadly projectiles. Innocent people could get hurt and of course, there's also the fact that bystanders aren't exactly psychologically prepared to witness supernatural activity. The people in this city experience enough traumas during morning rush-hour. I'd like to spare them from seeing stuff that will make grinding through traffic gridlock on the Deerfoot Trail seem like a pleasant drive in the country by comparison."

Marcus took a swig of his Coke and grimaced. "So we need to do this in an open space and secluded enough that it won't attract any unnecessary attention."

"Pretty much," I said. "Any thoughts on a location?"

Marcus chewed away at the end of his straw for a few seconds and said, "Calgary's a pretty congested city. We could do Nose Hill Park, seeing as how it's nothing but empty prairie for miles, but it's a known hang-out for the romantic crowd."

"Okay scratch that one," I said.

"It has to be either the north or south side of town and easy enough to find. I'm thinking the Calgary Rugby Stadium off Shepard Road. It's nowhere near as big as Nose Hill, but it's in an industrial block and absolutely nobody goes there at night."

I nodded in agreement. "Okay, we've got a location. Now all I have to do is commit my dad's grimoire to memory and we're good to go."

Marcus arched a wary eyebrow. "Can't you just... I don't know, make a cheat sheet or something?"

"That's pretty much what I'm going to have to do," I said, flipping through the book. "I also think we need to create a duel environment that favours us."

"What do you mean?"

I pointed to a page with a series of sketches showing what the grimoire described as 'defensive traps'. "I'm going to have to somehow separate the spirit of Matthew Hopkins from Hudibras and there are about five different kinds of rings that can be used to hold him in place."

"What about Hudibras?" asked Marcus as he examined the sketches. "How do you take him down?"

I exhaled heavily and said, "It will come down to a battle of wills and whose magic is stronger. I think he could be severely weakened if we can yank Hopkins out of him."

"But your dad said this guy was probably possessed by Hopkins. Doesn't that mean you have to do an–"

"Exorcism," I interrupted as I pointed to a paragraph long incantation in my father's handwriting. "A really complex one where if anything goes wrong, we're done like dinner."

Marcus shifted uncomfortably in his seat. "Gotcha, so do we head over to the rugby field now?"

"Not yet," I said, trying to banish the bleak tone from my voice. "We need to go to my house to get everything ready."

*Chapter 22*

The bus ride to the university C-Train station took less than twenty minutes and we'd timed it perfectly. Our train to the south-side of town was waiting for us when we hopped off the bus. Marcus sat next to me in a near-empty car. A cool breeze blew in from one of the opened windows and I had a few moments to collect my thoughts on how best to proceed in confronting Hudibras.

What tugged at me was how I'd been living in the dark for so long. I'd gone from a seemingly harmless intervention on behalf of a little old biddy and her cat to a life-and-death battle with a spirit holding a four hundred year-old grudge. Everything that happened in the past two days shook my beliefs as a witch and left me wondering whether once this was over, I'd swear off witchcraft all together and live a quiet life in the relative safety and security of anonymity.

Yeah, like that would ever happen.

I spun the copper band around my left wrist and I

considered the facts as I knew them. Hudibras saw me as a threat. The spirit of Matthew Hopkins was either in possession of Hudibras or they had come to some kind of dark bargain. My father was a Shadowcull in life and I carried his bloodline which made me an automatic target. Someone who worshipped the Left Hand Path had him killed and now that I'd taken his place as a Shadowcull, they'd be gunning for me. But why go after my mom now? She'd spent her life protecting me from danger; why not get her – and me – earlier. Was my father's death and my impending showdown with Hudibras connected somehow, or not?

I watched the houses zipping by as the train hummed along and I wondered for a short moment, what life would be like if I'd never been a witch. Would I have any interest in the comings and goings of people my age? I glanced at Marcus from the corner of my eye. Would I have even noticed that such a fantastic guy like Marcus existed?

Probably not. I'd no doubt build my life around attaining popularity at school or landing the hottest boyfriend like all the other drone-girls. I'd be more interested in clothes and what my social circle was up to and I'd probably insert the word 'like' into every second sentence.

Still, it *would* be cool to have a circle of friends that weren't on the fringe. I'm only human and it was natural that I'd desire what the popular people at school had. What teenager doesn't? Why shouldn't I want to be the center of attention instead of having to practice a craft that I couldn't share with anyone outside of Mom and Marcus? I couldn't even imagine what a normal life looked like and a big part of me wanted one now more than ever.

Ugh.

I pushed the notion of a life outside of witchcraft and geekdom out of my head. My school is filled with geeks just like Marcus and me and so what if we're not in that ten percent of the school population that's popular? I'm a witch; Marcus is a freaking Einstein doppelganger clone of uber brilliance and every other geek at my school rocks. Period.

Take that all you boring 'beautiful' people.

I exhaled slowly and reeled my thoughts back in to what I had to do in the next few hours. Speculating about a life outside of witchcraft or the reasons why fate had chosen me in its warped and self-amusing way was pointless. Time was short and I had to help Mom. Soon.


We got back to my house shortly after 1am where we were met by an enormous Great Dane that was sitting on the front step like it was expecting us.

"That's a big dog," Marcus whispered, as if he didn't want to anger the beast. "Think Hudibras sent a canine to take you down?"

The dog sneezed, and then stood up. It cocked its head a couple of times, and then it opened its mouth.

"Relax, it's only me," the dog said in a deep, baritone voice.

Marcus jumped back about ten feet and nearly stumbled into one of Mom's weed beds. "Whoa! That freaking dog can talk!"

The Great Dane trotted down the steps and grabbed the strap of my backpack with its black muzzle. It sniffed at the copper band on my left wrist and then let out a huge sneeze that sent a spray of dog snot all over my arm.

"Gross!" I said. "Betty, you freaking body-snatched a *dog*?"

"He was the only thing I could find," said Betty the dog. "So don't start on me about the choice of forms I take. This mutt was on death row at the pound so if anything, I'm doing him a favour."

Marcus approached Betty with a good measure of trepidation, then reached out and scratched behind her pointy ears. "At least you didn't show up on Julie's doorstep as a French Poodle," he said.

Betty the dog lurched forward and pushed her enormous head into Marcus' midsection, knocking him back into the weed bed.

"That, young man, is not funny," her voice rumbled. "Julie, I'm sure by now that you've been in contact with your father. You've learned something about your past, I take it?"

I pushed Betty's huge, floppy head aside and stomped up the path to the front door. I whispered a word of magic and felt the sentinels surrounding my house draw back enough for the three of us to enter. "Yeah, well it would have been really nice if you'd told me about him from the start. While you were at it, you could have told me about Shadowculls and coven justice, too."

She trotted up the walk and stepped into the house with Marcus following close behind. "As I said before; I can't offer information, I can only answer questions. Had you asked, I would have told you everything."

I waved my right index finger and the door slammed behind Marcus and Betty the Great Dane. I could feel the sentinels engage and I knew that for the time being, we'd be safe if Hudibras decided to come after me in my own house. No sooner had I armed the sentinels than the phone in the living room rang. The caller ID said it was from the Rockeyview Hospital and a sickly feeling washed over me as I picked the receiver up from the cradle.

"H-hello?" I said quietly.

"This is Evelyn Abrams from the Rockyview Hospital—I'm the charge nurse on the intensive care unit. I'm calling for Julie Richardson."

My throat was dry. "This is Julie – is everything okay? Did something happen to my mom?"

"Approximately forty-five minutes ago your mom experienced a seizure." The nurse's voice was calm but I didn't detect any reassurance in her tone. "We've stabilized for the time being and we're running some tests to determine the cause. Unfortunately, the more serious issue is that her kidneys are beginning to fail."

"Her kidneys? Is she going to be okay?" I asked, barely choking out the words.

"The best we can do right now, Julie, is to keep your mom stable. The tests should give us some indication as to why she had a seizure; our concern is that her kidneys are shutting down. The doctors are doing everything they can and we just wanted to give you an update on her condition. Will you be at this number?"

I bit hard into my right knuckle; it was everything I could do to keep myself from screaming. "Yes," I said, quietly. "Thank you for calling."

The living room was dead silent as I hung up the phone.

"Is everything okay?" Marcus asked.

My head was throbbing as I fought back the urge to throw up. I'm no medical expert, but I'd watched enough TV to know that when a person's kidney's go it's a sign that eventually all their organs will fail. When that happens, death happens. I instinctively wanted to hop on the C-Train and head to the hospital to be with her, because if she was dying, then she deserved to have a loved one at her side to be there for her. There was still a chance that I could save her but the window of opportunity was closing quickly. Mom was running out of time and I had to end this, there was simply no other way to save her life.

"We have a ton of stuff to do and not much time to

do it," I said firmly. "Mom's taken a turn for the worse. I'm going to battle it out with Hudibras tonight and I absolutely *have* to defeat him. Failure isn't an option."

Betty wagged her tail and it thumped loudly against the side of the sofa. "And I believe that you can do this, Julie. You wear the weapon of a Shadowcull. This gives you a significant advantage."

"Maybe he doesn't know she's a Shadowcull," Marcus interrupted. "He might be under the impression that Julie is just a very skilled witch."

"It doesn't matter at this point what Hudibras thinks," I said as I headed down the stairs to the library. "I have a grimoire filled with the tools of the trade for a Shadowcull; I just need to formulate a plan of attack."

And I needed to make it the mother of all magical attacks. The good news was that Betty had an encyclopaedic knowledge of the arcane and my head was swimming with questions to ask. She'd earn her pay – or at least a milk bone – before I was done.

I stepped into the library and placed the grimoire on the work table. "Betty, what do you know about bindings? My dad's grimoire lists a bunch of them that can be used as something he calls quick magic."

Two enormous forepaws appeared on the edge of the work table as Betty the dog stood on her hind legs to get a better view of my father's grimoire. "Obviously you know the central purpose of a binding spell. I suspect your intent is to bind the practitioner to your will."

I nodded. "Kind of. We figured out that Matthew Hopkins may be in possession of Hudibras' body and possibly even his subconscious. We need to figure out a way to bind Hudibras in place long enough to conduct an exorcism."

Betty stretched out a ridiculously long pink tongue from between a set of floppy black lips and licked her chops. "The most powerful form of exorcism is by use of the Roman Ritual," she said with a loud smack. "Unfortunately we're not dealing with a creature from the abyss."

"There's something in here called a 'strain binding'," I said. "What's that about?"

Betty leaned in and I assumed she was scanning the page. "That might work, actually. It's a kind of binding spell that draws its power not only from the will of the spell caster, but also from the target."

"That sounds like it would be powerful enough to bind Hudibras long enough to conduct an exorcism." Marcus said as he cleared a space on the work table.

Betty the dog grunted. "That depends on the will of the person invoking the spell. I suspect that despite your relative inexperience, Julie, your Shadowcull's band would certainly compensate."

I grabbed a felt marker and wrote the invocation on my left forearm. Yeah, I was making a cheat but it didn't matter. I needed to have an edge. "And the exorcism itself – what do you recommend?"

Betty got down from the table and stretched with a

loud groan. "I should think a standard exorcism would suffice, but you'll need to craft a vessel to contain the spirit of Matthew Hopkins. I'd recommend a funeral urn or something similar, preferably made from copper."

"Why not use the box from the cemetery?" Marcus asked. "I remember your Dad's ghost saying it was copper and covered with sigils that were all spells of some kind."

I span around. "Marcus, you're a genius! That's exactly what we'll use. Would you go upstairs and grab it out of my backpack?"

Marcus grinned from ear to ear. "I'm on it."

I returned to the worktable and flipped through Dad's grimoire again. "Marcus is out of earshot, Betty. I'm going to use my father's black curse if I have to."

Betty the dog cocked her head to the right either as a display of confusion or general concern, I wasn't sure which. "You're certain you wish to invoke a black curse, Julie? Surely you're not expecting Hudibras might kill you."

"It could happen," I said grimly. "If I'm going down, so will Hudibras, and I have no problem at all laying a black curse onto him. If my death means that my mom gets to live, then it's a fair trade as far as I'm concerned."

Betty the dog shuffled over to the shelf and nudged at a clear Tupperware box containing a fine white powder that resembled sugar. She grabbed it between her powerful jaws and brought it over to the table. "You won't need a black curse," the giant dog said.

"This is 'ember's salt', or what is commonly known as 'witch's chaff'."

"And that would be…?"

"A magical countermeasure," she continued. "Just like the chaff that pilots use to jam the guidance capabilities of missiles, witch's chaff can jam someone's magic if you get enough of it on their body. We just need something to act as a delivery device. It would be nice if we had some pyrotechnics."

Marcus came back into the library and slid the copper box across the work table. "Did someone say something about pyrotechnics?"

I nodded. "Yeah. We've got something we need to launch at Hudibras. Any ideas?"

Marcus' lips turned up into a smile so large I thought his face might crack. "How about an arsenal worth of firecrackers?"

I could have kissed him. "You've got firecrackers on you?"

"Nope, but we've got a box full of 'em in the garage at my house. We were going to use them on Canada Day, but we got rained out. Can you use your magic to light them?"

I made a small effort of will and snapped my fingers. A tiny blue flame flickered brightly from the center of my palm. "Does that answer your question?"

Marcus beamed. "Okay *sweet*, and that is *really* freaking cool, Julie. I'll run home and be back in less than twenty minutes."

"That sounds good to me," I said with a hint of optimism. "I'll walk you to the door so I can disarm the sentinels and then Betty and I can figure out how to lace those firecrackers."

## Chapter 23

I mixed the ember's salt in a large mortar and pestle. Betty said to lace it with something that would act as a kind of glue, and the only thing I could think of was a pouch of powdered glue, the kind you mix with water. If it worked, the powdered glue would enhance the ember's salt to such an extent that it would cling to not only Hudibras, but whatever kind of corporeal form Matthew Hopkins would take once I conducted the exorcism. I uttered a strong word of magic to unite the two ingredients and then sprinkled a handful into my father's copper box as a backup in case the spirit of Matthew Hopkins was somehow able to evade the multiple binding spells I'd invoked into the engravings on the box.

I dumped the entire contents of the ember's salt into a large ceramic bowl and waited for Marcus to show up. Betty had disappeared for a few moments and returned with a blanket that dangled from her drooling doggy lips. She dropped it at my feet and let out a loud sneeze, once again covering me with dog snot.

Oh yeah, being a witch rocks sometimes.

"What's that?" I asked, poking at the blanket with my left foot.

Betty stepped back and dropped onto her tan coloured haunches. "I found it in a box on a shelf in your mother's closet. I picked up the scent of your father's residual magic on that copper box and it led me to this."

"What is it?"

"A Shadowcull's cloak," she said. "It has protective spells sewn into the fabric and it's strong enough to stop everything from bullets to hellfire. You'd best wear it."

I reached for the cloak and felt it tingling with magical energies. As my fingers brushed against the thick fabric, a pattern of complex sigils and runes glowed for a short moment and then dissolved back into the cloak. I picked it up and held it out for inspection. It was the blackest fabric I'd ever seen, so black the light from the desk lamp beside me couldn't penetrate it. I threw it over my shoulders and was nearly whacked in the eye by a copper chain with a perfectly round clasp that bore my father's mark. I hooked the clasp in a thick canvas loop. The cloak dropped down past my knees.

"Don't forget the hood," Betty rumbled.

"Right," I said, reaching back and pulling the hood over my head. It fell over my eyes and I was enveloped in a warm blanket of my father's will, not to mention some butt-kicking protection.

"You look very much the Shadowcull," said Betty the dog. "The enemy is going to be in for a shock when he lays eyes on you."

I lowered the hood and blinked at her for a moment. "Betty, I need a few minutes to myself. There's something I have to do before we duke it out with Hudibras."

The giant dog nodded once and plodded off to the living room. "Very well, I'll keep an eye out for Marcus."

I grabbed a stick of chalk and drew a circle on the kitchen floor and stepped inside. I took a deep breath and then knelt down and pulled the hood over my head as I closed my eyes and raised my magic.

I concentrated as I reached for my peripheral focus and within seconds, I felt my spirit once again slingshot out at breakneck speed. The neighbourhood of Lake Sundance flew past me in a blur of light and sound as I flew over treetops and buildings. I soared over the Glenmore Reservoir, past sailboats tied to their moorings and over Glenmore Park. I zipped through the roof of the Rockyview hospital. I whisked through three floors and then past a nurse's station until I was looking down on my mother and when I saw her, my heart stopped.

There was an intravenous bag hanging from a stand next to the bed. A tube led to a pump that beeped every few seconds as it delivered tiny drips intravenously to her body through a needle taped to her right hand. I felt my heart breaking as I reached out and suddenly I could see the vaporous form of my hand brushing gently against her cheek. I leaned in to whisper in her ear.

"Mom," I said, pushing back the urge to start crying. "I love you so much and I'm so damned sorry for dragging you into all of this. I wish it were me lying there instead of you because you've always been the strong one. You've always been there for me – from the time that Dad died and through my whole life up to now. And I saw him, Mom – I saw Dad. I spoke with him. He told me why you've been protecting me ever since he died. I know that someone took him from us and now someone wants to take you from me, but I'm not going to let that happen. I've taken his place as a Shadowcull and I'm going to fight with everything I've got to save you... To save us. I don't know if you can hear me or feel me, Mom, but please hang on. Don't give up, okay? You've never given up on me in my whole life and I'm not about to give up on you. I just need a few more hours, so please hang on."

I looked on her for another few moments when I felt the sentinels warn me of someone approaching the house. Instantly my spirit left the hospital room and I was alone in the kitchen. I quickly got back to my feet and in seconds I was peering through the peephole on the front door. It was Marcus. His backpack bulged over his right shoulder. I whispered a word of magic and lowered the sentinels enough to let him in the house.

Marcus' eyes bugged out when he saw me in the cloak. "Whoa! You look like a *Jedi*."

I pulled back the hood. "And I'm strong with the

ways of the Force."

Marcus trotted into the house and handed me a backpack stuffed with enough firecrackers to put a man in orbit. "We've got enough pyro in here for an artillery barrage," he said.

"Did you wake your parents?" I asked as I closed the door and rearmed the sentinels.

He snorted. "Not a chance. My dad snores so loud that he can drown out low-flying aircraft."

I motioned for Marcus to follow me back down the stairs to Mom's library. I glanced at my watch and saw that it was 1.45am. Sunrise wouldn't be until shortly before 7am, but people started heading for work in the industrial blocks of Calgary around 5am. That gave us a little more than three hours to take down Hudibras.

Betty the dog was up on her hind legs again reading my father's grimoire as I dropped the backpack beside the ceramic bowl filled with witch's chaff. I had enough sense to spot a box of zip lock bags on the shelving unit and I gave a hopeful smile. "Marcus, grab those zip lock bags, I have an idea."

"No problemo," he said, tossing me box. "What's your plan?"

I caught the box with one hand and ripped open the top. "We're going to stuff each bag with the firecrackers and make a kind of grenade out of them. I figure we can concentrate the effectiveness of the witch's chaff that way."

"Sounds good. What do you want me to do?"

I pointed to the ceramic bowl. "Coat all the firecrackers with the chaff. I'm going to run upstairs and take a quick shower just to make sure none of the chaff's residue is on my body. The last thing I need is for my magic to be weakened in the heat of the duel."

The shower felt heavenly and I wondered for a moment if this might be the last shower I'd ever take.

But only for a moment.

I was very near the end of my quest to save Mom and while I was fully aware that I might not survive the next few hours, I was filled with a curious mixture of optimism and a strong desire for revenge. In the short span of a day and a half, Hudibras had turned my life upside-down and I aimed to take it out on his hide.

You know, *assuming* my magic was strong enough.

I glanced down at my Shadowcull's band as the hot water splashed down my shoulders. I had my amulet, my copper band, a vessel to capture Matthew Hopkins' spirit and some magical countermeasures that would weaken Hudibras. All that was left for me to do was to send a clear message into the night by means of a summoning spell and it would be up to skill, fate and a little bit of luck after that.

I shut the water off and stepped out of the shower to dry myself. I should have been terrified about what I was about to do, but the attacks on me and those I loved fuelled a simmering anger and a desire to strike back.

And I was starting to like this new, dark side to me.

I hung up my towel on the back of the door and ran a comb through my damp hair. Marcus had stood by me, God love him, just like he said he would. It made sense for me to ask that he go home and wait to hear from me, but I knew that would fall on deaf ears. He'd already had a near-death experience tonight and it only acted to reinforce his resolve to be there for me, even when I was being a high maintenance you-know-what.

Minutes later, I was back down in the lab when I noticed my laptop was still open. I walked over and was about to shut it down when I saw the flickering image of the end of the YouTube video showing the attack on those poor dogs. I clicked on the browser icon and saw that I had a notice in my toolbar informing me that I had email. I clicked on the icon and found a message in my inbox from Marcus. From the time stamp, it looked like he'd sent it after I shot him down in the basement the other day.

I squinted at the header, it said: "Just read this, okay?"

So I did.

*Julie:*

*I've decided to write you an email so that I can explain what happened in your basement today. Call me a wuss for not telling you how I feel in person, but that didn't exactly go over terribly well when I tried. For the record, I said you were beautiful and meant every word of it.*

*I did this because it's how I've felt for a very long time now and I wanted you to know how I felt – how I've always felt about you. It was a conscious choice on my part and I did it knowing full well that you probably don't see me in the same way that I see you. That's fine – that's a risk a person has to take when they want to tell someone how much they mean to them. And you mean so much to me, Julie. Not because you have weird-ass powers that fascinate and terrify me all at the same time. Not because we've been best friends since we were little kids. It's just that I care about you in a way that is more than friendship. I miss you when you're not around – like when you and your mom go on vacation. I've had to stop myself from reaching out to take your hand or to just kiss you because I don't want to get hurt by the most important person in my life. I mean, nobody wants to face rejection and I know there's a real chance that when you read this, you'll want to send me packing because you don't feel the way I do.*

*Still, it's a risk I'm willing to take because… well, I love you.*

*There, I said it. I love you and I've been in love with you for a long time now. I just haven't had the courage to tell you – again, that whole rejection thing. I know you might be trying to figure out a way to let me down easy or to tell me that you like me as a friend and I'm sort of bracing myself for it. Just know that regardless of how you feel about me, I do love you very much.*

   *I think that I always will.*
         *Marcus*


I allowed myself a long and very heart-wrenching sigh. I held my hand over the keyboard and bit my lip hard because I wanted to email him back in case things went badly at the Rugby Stadium. But I couldn't. I needed to stay focused on taking down Hudibras.

Still, it *was* a beautiful letter. It also put to rest any fears that I had about Marcus being into Marla and I wished I'd seen it before I decided to get mega-bitchy with the both of them. I felt tears welling up as I re-read the email. Every single word was a declaration of the joy that Marcus felt whenever he was near me. Nobody had ever expressed anything so loving and genuine to me before in my life. My head was swimming with emotions that bounced against the interior walls of my skull at about a million miles an hour because for the first time I realized how much I actually *meant* to someone. Marcus really and truly loved me with all his heart. *Me!* He hadn't abandoned me. And he was *still* by my side even now when the likelihood of my death was staring me straight in the face.

Tears rolled down my cheeks and a hollow ache radiated out from the center of my chest. I gulped air again as I ran my sleeve across my face to wipe away the tears when it finally dawned on me.

Whoa. I was in love with Marcus Guffman.

I wanted to race downstairs and throw my arms around him. I wanted to whisper in Marcus' ear that I loved him too, that I'd read his letter and that he'd touched my heart, but I couldn't. I had to keep my mind on defeating Hudibras. I had to fight. I absolutely *had* to bloody win.

I didn't have any choice.

I decided that when all this was over, I'd tell Marcus that I'd read his letter and that I loved him with all my heart. I'd apologize for treating the one person who'd never stopped believing in me like shit and that I wouldn't have come this far if it hadn't been for him.

All I had to do was to survive the night and save my mother's life.

## Chapter 24

Marcus was wiping his hands on a tea towel and there were twenty-one bags of witch's chaff-laced firecrackers all lined up and ready to go. It took everything in my power to stop myself from taking his hand and telling him that I had read his letter. But this wasn't the time or place.

Betty's tail thumped agreeably when she saw me walk into the room. I was dressed in a pair of hiking boots, black cargo pants and a thin, black sweater that clung to my curves like plastic wrap. I think Marcus noticed too because his face turned three kinds of red after he took one look at me.

"Marcus, you're going to be in charge of launching those bags at Hudibras," I said firmly. "Stuff them in your backpack and when we get to the rugby field, we'll find a good place for you to hide."

"This may sound dumb, Julie, but will I be protected?" he asked.

"Yes and no," I said uneasily. "I'm not familiar with

the layout of the field, but I'm going to assume there's only one set of gates. I think that's where we start launching the chaff. If there's enough time, I'll have a circle for you that will offer protection from anything Hudibras sends your way. Of course if something bad happens to me, make sure you high-tail it out of there and head for the hills."

Betty the dog's baritone voice rumbled. "Marcus should stay with me. Don't forget that my magic can also pack a punch when I choose to use it."

I scratched Betty's thick muscular chest and knelt down. "I didn't think it would be right for you to get involved. This is my grudge match, not yours."

Betty leaned her giant head into my shoulder and nuzzled me affectionately. "I am your guardian and part of my job is to protect you if you're in danger. But I can't fight this battle for you because you issued the challenge for this duel. You're a Shadowcull now, Julie; it falls on you to defeat Hudibras."

I stroked her shining tan coat. "Yeah. I just hope I've got enough in me to do it, you know?"

She nodded and stepped back a couple of feet. "Just remember to channel your emotions. Shape them into the most devastating magic you can muster and don't let Hudibras know you're intimidated, not even a breath of fear."

"I'll remember that, Betty," I said firmly. "Everyone ready to go?"

Marcus glanced at Betty and then back to me

and said, "Uh, sure... there's only one problem."

"What's that?" I asked.

Marcus shrugged hard. "There's no bus service in Calgary at two in the morning and we can't call a cab because the cabbie will get suspicious since they don't generally drop teenagers off in Calgary's industrial block when the entire city is sound asleep."

Shit. I'd forgotten about that.

I turned to Betty and offered an awkward smile.

She snorted. "I have paws, and I doubt my long legs will reach the pedals... You get to drive your mother's car, but I'll make sure it gets us there in one piece."

"Just don't get a scratch on it or she'll kill me," I warned.

Betty let out an aristocratic sniff as she turned and headed up the stairs. I gave Marcus a hopeful smile and when his eyes met mine, I actually blushed a little bit.

Marcus held up both our backpacks for my inspection. "I've got the pyro in my bag and all your stuff including your father's grimoire is inside yours. I wish I could be of more use but–"

I grabbed my bag and said, "Marcus, look, I want you to know that I wouldn't have been able to come this far without you. Whatever happens, just know that you've been rock solid through all this. Let's head outside so I can call out Hudibras and get my mom back."

The three of us to headed outside to the shed. It seemed only fitting that I should call out Hudibras from the site of his first attack on me. I ran my finger along the twisted hinges that were the only thing remaining of the door. Betty and Marcus stood alongside the marble circle where my mom exorcised the spirit inside the teddy bear. It was time to do some serious magic.

I stepped into the circle and knelt down. I touched the smooth cold marble ring and drew on a small amount of my spirit and whispered, "Seek."

The ring hummed with magical energies as I pulled out a piece of chalk from my pants pocket and began writing my message to Hudibras using the Theban alphabet so there would be no mistake as to who the message was coming from. When I was done, I stood up and stretched out my arms and I searched for Hudibras' magical signature through the supercharged atmosphere. I intensified my focus, and closed my eyes tight. I sensed the familiar magical signatures of local practitioners whose energies brushed against my skin, and within seconds, I felt weightless as my spirit drifted through thick fields of magic, both good and malicious. To my surprise, the energies parted, as if sensing my purpose. Force of every description divided like an endless sea of curtains, each pulling back to make way for my will to seek out the now familiar pulse of Hudibras' own malicious intent.

I'd homed in on it now, an inky blot floating amid of a haze of spectral blues and reds; his magical signature stained the supernatural realm with an old simmering hatred for me, for all witches. It knew I was coming as it bubbled and frothed in my presence. I drew upon my message written and I hurled my own menacing, vengeful words into the middle of the boiling mass. It hit with amazing force, a geyser of dark magic spewed up, and I knew my message had been received when a cold emotionless voice rang out, "To your doom, witch. Tonight you will breathe your last."

The three of us hopped into Mom's car and I turned the key. The engine roared to life and I stared at the steering wheel for a moment as I tried to remember how to turn on the headlights.

"Okay," I said with a huff. "I can do this. Betty, where's the lights?"

Betty's poked her huge head between the front seats and said, "The lights are that little knob just above your left hand. Pull it toward you and then put the car in reverse. All you need to do is get it backed onto the street and slip it into drive, I can do the rest."

I nodded and rested my sweaty right palm on the shift knob and pulled it back until I saw that it was in reverse. The car shot backwards, tyres squealing as I swung the steering wheel hard to the right.

"Take your foot off the gas pedal!" Betty snapped. "Just pump the brake!"

I did as instructed and slowly navigated the car back out of our driveway and onto the street. I straightened the tyres and kept my foot on the brake pedal as I switched the car into drive.

Betty closed her brown eyes for half a second and whispered something completely incomprehensible. I gripped the steering wheel so tightly my knuckles were turning white.

"You can remove your hands from the wheel and take your foot off the brake," she said. "The car knows where it needs to go now. Might I suggest a veil so that either the police or Hudibras won't see us coming?"

I exhaled slowly and slipped my copper amulet into the recess of my Shadowcull's band. I closed my eyes and whispered words of magic, drawing the veil over the car like a crisp, clean sheet on a mattress. Within seconds we were rolling down my street and amazingly, Betty's magic ensured the car stayed within the speed limit.

Marcus fidgeted in the passenger seat next to me and I could tell he was frightened, so I placed a reassuring hand on his.

"Are you scared?" he whispered.

I tried to offer something resembling a hopeful smile and squeezed his hand. "Shitless," I replied. "I'd be lying if I said I wasn't, Marcus. And you know what? If either of us weren't scared, they might as well ship us off to a padded room somewhere."

He nodded "Who do you think Hudibras is?"

I shrugged hard as the car whipped onto Deerfoot Trail and accelerated to sixty miles an hour. "We're about to find out."

"Yeah," he said. "Listen Julie, you look wicked hot in that Jedi outfit."

A big goofy grin washed over my face and I let out a huge belly laugh. "You wait until *now* to tell me that I'm hot?"

He snorted. "Can't help it. You're dead sexy."

"It's a Shadowcull's cloak," I said, half smiling. "Not quite as subtle as that of a Jedi Knight, but way more kickass."

Betty the dog let out a loud cough from the back seat. "Let's keep our heads in the game," she warned. "Julie, do you sense that Hudibras received your message?"

"Loud and clear," I said firmly. "Any thoughts on how we're going to take him out besides chucking bags of firecrackers at him?"

Marcus reached into his pack and pulled out an honest to goodness slingshot. I could have kissed him. "While you're peppering him with magic, I thought I could launch the bags at him with this. I've also got about two thousand ball bearings for good measure."

"Can you shoot that thing with accuracy?" I asked.

Marcus snorted again. "Puh-lease! Firing a slingshot is a matter of anticipating the trajectory, compensating for wind and applying the right amount of force – in short, science."

"Smart move, Marcus," I said. "When I give you the word, you fire the chaff and hopefully it will work. We'll bean him with ball bearings as a distraction."

We coasted onto the exit ramp leading to Glenmore Trail and I cracked open the window for a breath of fresh air. My stomach was doing backflips as the certainty of the deadly confrontation started hitting home. Everything up to this point spoke of menace and dark magic and sure, I'd successfully withstood two attacks from Hudibras, but I couldn't help but wonder if he had been holding back somehow. My instincts told me that everything about the two attacks was intended to kill me and that Hudibras was using the full measure of his power, but call me superstitious, if he was half as clever as I thought he'd be, I was certain Hudibras had a backup plan somewhere.

I just needed to be that much smarter and faster.

Mom's car was cruising along Shepard Road and I could see the billboard-sized sign advertising the Calgary Rugby Union less than a block away. I reached out with my magic to feel if Hudibras was nearby and felt nothing, so I assumed it was safe to pull into the parking lot. We came to an abrupt halt in the parking spot nearest the main gate and I let out a nervous breath.

I looked around the parking lot for any cars and all I could see were a few dozen squashed Tim Horton's coffee cups and a plastic bag rolling across the pavement in the breeze. I took another nervous breath and turned to Betty and Marcus.

"Okay listen, Hudibras may already be here and if he is, he's probably using a veil. Betty, can you sniff one out and let me know?"

The big dog nodded once. "Yes I can, and if I detect one, we'll have to move very quickly to set up a defence."

"I'll draw magic circles all over that field," I said, patting the hip pocket of my black cargo pants. "I've got lots of chalk. Marcus, I want you to stick close to me when we hop out of the car because we're going to run like heck to the main gate."

"Right. I'm glue. Gotcha," Marcus said in a surprisingly firm voice.

I took a last look around the parking lot and opened the door. "Okay everyone," I said resolutely. "Let's do this."

## Chapter 25

I tore across the parking lot and leaped over a concrete barrier fetching up under a huge arch that led to the main gate. Marcus was on my tail and Betty galloped like a clumsy gazelle, her thick black lips flapping in the breeze.

"So far so good," I whispered, as we ducked behind a stack of plastic trash cans. "Betty, can you sense a veil?"

The big dog was panting now, her huge pink tongue pulled back and forth in her giant mouth. She licked her chops. "Nothing that I can detect," she said between pants. "He's not here yet."

I poked my head around the trash cans and gazed through the chain link gate. There were two enormous stacks of red and blue bleachers alongside the field and I spotted a tractor hitched to a huge rolling grass cutter. I clenched my jaw and decided it was too obvious a target for Marcus to start launching the witch's chaff from, so the safest and most effective way to employ

Marcus would be for him to constantly switch firing positions beneath the bleachers in hope it would provide some cover.

"Okay, this is where we part company," I said firmly. "I'm going to hex the lock and throw open the gate. As soon as I'm done, Betty and I will run into the center of the field and I'll set up a magic circle in case we need to fall back. Marcus, I want you to take the bags of witch's chaff and scoot underneath the bleachers. I'll signal you when I want you to start launching them and make certain you see where I draw the circle because if things go badly that's the Alamo, got it?"

Marcus threw his arms around me and squeezed. "Understood. Julie, be careful, okay?"

I hugged him back and gave him a gentle bonk on the forehead. "We can do this," I said softly. "You can do this, Marcus."

I stood up and pointed at the large padlock and whispered, "*Hexus*". There was a spray of fine sparks and the lock fell to the ground, dragging a length of chain with it. I gave a last glance of confirmation to Betty and Marcus and pushed the gate open with a tiny effort of magic. They swung wide, their squeaking hinges cutting through the silence of the night like a blade through flesh.

"Go!" I whispered, and Marcus took off like an Olympic sprinter. I gathered my focus into a tight ball and reached out, looking for even the tiniest trace of dark magic. The only thing I felt was the beating of my heart and warmth of Betty the dog next to me, so I scrambled ahead until I was in the center of the rugby field. I laid flat on the ground, kind of a dumb idea given that I had a one-thirty pound Great Dane standing next to me, but it was instinctive. I held my breath and listened only to hear Marcus scuttling between the long steel poles holding up the bleachers. If Hudibras was here, he had a hell of a veil.

"What do you think, Betty?" I whispered.

The big dog dropped onto its belly and stared straight at the gates. "I think you need to get that circle drawn as quickly as possible. I'll keep an eye out for the enemy."

"Good plan," I said, reaching into my pocket and pulling out a thick rectangular stick of white chalk. I dropped my backpack beside Betty and ran about twenty feet behind her, then reached down and started tracing my circle onto the cool turf.

"Hurry!" Betty half-growled.

"I'm just about done!" I said, as I completed the irregular circle. I did a quick scan of the bleachers and then dove back onto grass next to Betty. We lay in silence, the darkness of the rugby field made it near impossible to see beyond the bleachers, impossible for someone other than a Shadowcull, that is.

I could still hear Marcus and I spotted his aura flickering away like a candle. I reached into my backpack and pulled out my father's grimoire along with the copper box and stuffed them both in my other cargo pocket as we waited patiently for Hudibras to arrive.

It was 2.57am and my gut told me that Hudibras would make his presence known at the top of the hour. Why? Because three in the morning is the time of most deaths and the time of most births, look it up if you don't believe me. It marks the end of the three-hour period known as the witching hour and it is thought the end of the witching hour is when witches are most vulnerable.

But I wasn't most witches.

I wore the cloak and copper band of a Shadowcull and my instincts – a Shadowcull's instincts – told me that all hell was going to break loose in less than three minutes.

I took a deep breath and drew my hood over my head, then I stood up in the center of the circle. "Get ready, Marcus!" I called. My voice bounced off the bleachers and filled the stadium. I pulled back the thin black sleeves of my sweater to reveal my Shadowcull's band on my left wrist and the quick magic cheat I'd scrawled on my right forearm in permanent ink. Betty stood beside me and tensed as she sniffed the air while I adopted a defensive position and drew into my spirit for the battle to come.

And come it did.

Every single light in the stadium lit up like a thousand welders' torches and I shielded my eyes against the glare. The ground trembled beneath me and suddenly an ear-splitting screech echoed through the stadium. Betty's lips drew back and she raised her haunches as she let out a guttural growl. She dug her claws into the turf and hunched down, her pointy ears flattened against her skull, her gleaming white set of teeth bared.

What happened next made my blood freeze. A swirl of dirt and debris drew up from the ground into a spinning pillar, quickly morphing into a whirlwind's funnel. Oh yeah, Hudibras announced his presence by calling up a tornado that sent the huge metal gates flying a hundred feet in the air. The garbage cans we'd been crouching behind only moments earlier shot across the field like they'd been launched from a battery of cannon crashing into the turf and sending clumps of sod flying in all directions.

The explosion of twisting and twirling debris was deafening and I covered my ears to block out the noise. The spinning cloud of wind and deadly projectiles tore the first set of bleachers from their concrete footings, battering the red and blue seats until they were nothing more than sheets of twisted metal. I glanced at Marcus who raced below the second set of bleachers. He opened his backpack and pulled out the first bag of witch's chaff and then crouched low and took aim with his sling shot.

"Fire!" I shouted, and Marcus sent the bag of chaff directly in the path of the funnel cloud. I grated my teeth together and snarled a hex at the bag which immediately exploded in a multi-coloured flare of light.

A cloud of chaff-laced smoke was sucked into the lumbering vortex and it seemed to lose a small amount of momentum, so I threw a small binding spell at it and shouted for Marcus to launch another volley.

He fired again and I threw another hex at the bag of chaff. It exploded in another flare of light and I knew that I'd short-circuited Hudibras' spell. Now it was time to turn it back on him. I gathered together strands of white-hot magic, willing them together into a blast of energy that erupted from the tips of my outstretched fingers in four concentric rings of force. They buffeted the ground in front of the vortex sending, blasting through the alcove like a truck, smashing everything in its path. An enormous plume of thick brown dust blasted high into the air. Betty started barking like a rabid dog as I stretched out my hand to feel for Hudibras' location.

"He's on the move, Julie!" Betty howled. "Be on your guard!"

I hunched over to collect my breath. Repelling Hudibras' first attack had taken its toll, and I felt like someone had kicked me in the ribs and knocked the wind out of me.

The ground started shaking again as a flash of photo-negative light exploded through the alcove. Giant clumps of turf and gravel flew out in a wide arc and shot across the field. I braced myself for impact as I drew upon the power of my copper band and threw up a shield that ignited the air with a wall of Theban. The dirt and debris shattered into a shower of soil, blanketing the grass with earth. I coughed hard and Betty sneezed sending out a spray of dog snot and drool.

So far, I'd withstood everything that Hudibras had thrown at me, but fatigue was setting in and I had to do something to gain the upper hand because Hudibras could keep on pummelling me until I was too exhausted to defend myself. I couldn't physically see Hudibras, but I sensed his presence and gauging from the direction of his attack, he was probably at the entrance to the alcove. I decided that rather than wasting my energy, I'd take an unconventional approach and draw him out.

I stepped outside the magic circle and motioned for Betty to stay put. I pulled back the hood and brought my hands to the side of my face and started shouting for all I was worth.

> "'Has not this present Parliament
> A Lieger to the Devil sent,
> Fully impowr'd to treat about
> Finding revolted witches out
> And has not he, within a year,
> Hang'd threescore of 'em in one shire?
> Some only for not being drown'd,
> And some for sitting above ground,
> Whole days and nights, upon their breeches,
> And feeling pain, were hang'd for witches.'

"I know you're here, Matthew Hopkins and this is one witch who's going to kick your sorry ass before this night is over! Show yourself and face me you four-hundred year-old freak!"

An eerie calm descended on the rugby field. The only sound I could hear was the rush of the wind blowing through the bleachers and a panting Great Dane standing at my side.

But only for a moment. The sound of footsteps echoed across the concrete surface of the alcove as Hudibras cleared the gates and strode out onto the field.

And he was a *she*.

## Chapter 26

Betrayal is one of those crushing experiences in life that you never, *ever* see coming. It's always someone close to you who becomes a turncoat and you feel like they've kicked you in the stomach so hard that you can't even breathe. A poisonous rage mixed with the sting of humiliation surges through your veins and you wind up feeling like a complete idiot for having allowed yourself to fall victim to it. It's a slap in the face from someone you trusted. Someone you thought you knew. Someone who is so fucking clever they can hide their true intent right up until the very moment they stab you in the back.

I'd fully expected someone taller and definitely male. Instead, I stared across the field at none other than Marla Lavik, and from the glowing coals where her eyes were supposed to be, I could tell that Marla had left the building and wouldn't be coming back any time soon.

I'd known Marla since Junior High. We'd hung out

together; shared secrets together, schemed together and even dreamed together from time to time. I stood by her when her parents declared war on each other and she faced the custody battle from hell. I cried with her when she showed up on my doorstep after her mother refused to let her see her dad for what seemed like the hundredth time. I studied with her, went to the movies with her. Christ, my mom and I even took her to a spa on my fourteenth birthday and now she stood before me, her body vibrating with supernatural power.

But Marla wasn't a practitioner like me. True, she emitted the tiniest of magical signatures but if she had any abilities at all, I had always assumed they were probably of the Ouija board variety.

The kind of Ouija board a complete amateur uses when they're trying to summon a spirit.

I didn't have a clue what Marla had against me that would drive her to make a pact with a force like the spirit of Matthew Hopkins and it didn't matter. She'd just displayed an unimaginable level of power and that told me Marla was drawing on Matthew Hopkins' centuries-old hatred of witches to make her magic work. She just hadn't planned on winding up as his puppet when she summoned him and she probably didn't have a clue that the price of her pact might just be a shattered mind once this was all over.

And then it hit me.

The scorched symbol behind the toilet in the girls'

washroom. She'd summoned Hopkins' spirit in that bathroom stall just before all hell broke loose.

"That's my girlfriend!" I whispered to Betty. "That's Marla Lavik. She set me up!"

Betty the dog snorted. "She certainly dresses in a depressing fashion."

Marla had gone all out in her choice of wardrobe for our duel.

She was clad in a tight, black corset with a sheer black blouse, teamed with a pair of black hotpants beneath a leather trenchcoat. A pair of patent leather boots that gleamed under the bright lights of the field covered her legs up to her knees. Her jet-black hair was crimped and pulled back by a spider-shaped comb and her face was chalk white, with a thick coating of black lipstick on a pair of lips that wore a snarl.

And those eyes; they appeared nothing more than lifeless orbs set deep in her skull but the unearthly glow from where her pupils should have been told me that the spirit of Matthew Hopkins was somewhere inside and through her he intended to take me down.

"She's your friend, Julie," Betty the dog rumbled. "You need to get Hopkins out of her without killing the girl."

"Screw that! I want to tear her face off!" I snarled.

"Killing her will only lead you down a dark path," she warned. "So don't do it."

"She wants to kill me, Betty!" I snapped. "Or hadn't

you noticed that when the tornado ripped through the bleachers?"

Betty nudged my shoulder with her huge doggy head, smearing me with drool. "Save the girl's life, Shadowcull. Perhaps you will save her soul and your mother's while you're at it."

God damn it, I hate it when other people are right! It would have felt great to peel the skin from Marla's flesh but at the end of the day I'd be no better than the dark entity that was working through her. I'd been duped and humiliated by someone I called my friend, but I wasn't angry enough to kill. Talk about shitty justice. Marla hated me so much that she called up the spirit of Matthew Hopkins, stole my mother's soul and tried to kill me on four separate occasions in as many days and I had to be the good guy.

"Witchfinder General!" I shouted across the field. "Give me back my mother's soul or face the consequences!"

Marla cocked her head to the right and her snarl became a chilling, crooked smile. "Silence, hag!" she shouted, only it wasn't Marla's voice. Instead, she spoke in a male voice with a thick English accent. "My aim is to send you into the abyss!"

Okay, *nobody* calls me a hag and gets away with it. I raised my right arm and shouted, "Hit him with everything now, Marcus!"

A volley of witch's chaff landed with a series of soft thuds in front of Hopkins. I bellowed out a hex and each one exploded, filling the air around the Witchfinder General with a dense cloud of smoke until all I could see were the burning embers where Marla's eyes should have been.

Hopkins didn't even cough. Instead, he stepped through the wall of smoke as easily as someone stepping out of the shower and he made a lifting motion with his hands. Suddenly a row of buried sprinklers popped out of the ground and sprayed Hopkins with about a dozen or so cold jets of water.

"Underground sprinklers!" I groaned. "Why didn't I plan for that?"

Betty bared her teeth and started growling as Hopkins strode through the sprinklers, emerging about thirty feet away from me, dripping wet. I glanced at my wrist and threw one of my father's binding spells at Hopkins. He waved it aside as easily as waving away an annoying fly and it was at this point that I realized I was in big trouble.

"Ideas, Betty?" I whispered.

"I recommend some distraction and then a flanking of sorts," she said, motioning her enormous head toward the bleachers and Marcus.

"Hit her hard, Marcus!" I shrieked, as I made a beeline for the magic circle. Betty the dog tore across the field opposite me while Marcus started firing volley after volley of high velocity ball bearings at the body of Marla Lavik. Naturally this only fuelled Hopkins' rage and strengthened his magic, so I had to hit him with everything in me. I grated my teeth together and threw a blast of spectral force that nailed him square in the chest and sent Marla's body sailing through the air. I sensed static electricity in the atmosphere above and I drew my spirit into a giant hand that gathered the energy into a bolt of lightning that blasted out of the clouds like a giant, electrified sledgehammer. The earth exploded in front of Hopkins who was struggling to get back to his feet, so I set another ball of compressed force that streaked across the field like a bullet train.

Hopkins was prepared this time. He extended his arms and bellowed something that sounded like backwards English. My blast of force ricocheted off his magical shield and shot up into the sky like a rocket, and he wasn't done yet. His eyes blazed furiously as he spun around like a top, then as if on cue, every single light at the Calgary Rugby Union exploded in unison, sending out a lethal mixture of sparks and shards of glass in every direction. Darkness fell on the stadium like a death shroud, so I pulled my hood over my head and stretched out my hand to get a fix on Hopkins' magical signature.

Everything was silent for a moment as I intensified my focus. I reached out through the blackness, willing my power to pinpoint his location but I came up empty. I was just about to cast an illumination spell when I felt something hit me between the shoulder blades. There was a blinding flash for less than a second as the magical wards sewn into my cloak deflected the energy of the attack, but they did nothing to stop me from hurtling through the air. I landed in a heap next to a goalpost.

"The trouble with hags is they never realize their vile nature until the end," Hopkins' voice boomed across the empty field. "It's always that way when the guilty are about to be punished!"

I shook my head and coughed hard as I tried to get my bearings. I blinked a few times as I searched the darkness for Marla's form, but my instincts told me she was well hidden behind a shroud.

I got back to my feet and quickly gathered my magic. I spun around, sweeping my hands across my body as I sent out a wide crescent of emerald energy. It rolled across the empty field like a thunderhead, kicking up giant clumps of sod in its wake. I grunted agreeably at the display of my power and I was just about to fire off another salvo when I felt a sharp blow against the side of my head as searing pain drilled itself straight into the center of my brain. My neck snapped sharply to the right with such force I could have sworn I heard a loud crack. Instantly, my legs buckled beneath me and I dropped to the ground like a brick.

I don't know how long I was out for, but when I came to I had a mouth full of dirt and I gasped for air. I pushed myself up onto my hands, willing my legs to move but nothing happened. I grated my teeth together and pushed with all my strength as Betty's furious barking filled the empty stadium. There was a loud yelp followed by silence for a few seconds and then I heard the sound of Hopkins' boots strolling across the broken and battered turf of the stadium.

I pushed hard again, dragging myself behind the goalpost, as if the post itself could somehow protect me from Hopkins. Pain shot down my spine in fiery currents and tears welled up in my eyes. I rolled over onto my back and somehow managed to dig my heels into the ground – at least my back wasn't broken, but it might as well have been because whatever spell Hopkins nailed me with, it sapped my energy and I couldn't draw even the faintest trace of magic to protect myself.

Suddenly a ghostly blue glow pushed through the darkness and I saw the silhouette of Marla's body approaching. Hopkins' eyes burned through a misty haze of supernatural energy as he extended Marla's arms toward me. Her hands glowed with power. Her eyes narrowed and her lips twisted into a wicked smile. He was going to hit me with a death blow and there was absolutely nothing I could do about it. The air crackled and hummed with Hopkins' power as he opened his mouth. He was going to utter a death curse and that would be the end of Julie Richardson. I only hoped Marcus would get out alive.

"I-I'm sorry, Mom," I sobbed as tears stung my eyes.

"Now this ends, cursed witch!" Hopkins spat. His magic pulsed like a strobe light, becoming an enormous white ball of energy between Marla's outstretched hands. He drew Marla's arms over her shoulders and sneered.

He was about to let loose with the final blow when out of the corner of my eye I spotted a flash of movement.

*"Get the hell away from her!"* Marcus roared, as he threw himself at Marla's midsection like a linebacker. The force of his tackle sent Marla's body tumbling backwards while the ball of magic dropped onto Marcus like a five-hundred pound bomb.

"Marcus! No!" I screamed, as the torrent of black magic enveloped his entire body. He writhed in agony as the toxic curse worked its way up to his chest. A pair of ghostly hands reached out from the deathly shadow enveloping his body and hooked tightly around his neck, choking him with the skill of a serial killer.

And then something inside me snapped.

My Shadowcull's band lit up with magical energies, fuelling my body with the last reserves of my spirit. I sprung back to my feet as Hopkins readied another salvo of power to throw at me, but it was too little too late. His death curse was killing Marcus by inches with every passing second and the only way to save him was to destroy the spell's power at its source.

I lashed out at Hopkins, my fury supercharging my magic with emotional magic. I felt a wave of heat rush over my body as the darkness inside the stadium gave way to shimmering waves of colour. Marla shielded her eyes from the dazzling radiance pulsing from my body, then her body shot ten feet into the air as I lashed a binding onto Hopkins' spirit.

"Release Marcus from your spell or I'll tear your spirit to shreds!" I snarled.

Even though my binding had seized Hopkins like a bear trap, he remained defiant. "Your kind were a scourge four hundred years ago, hag! I was so good at my task that even now, in death, I do the noble work of not suffering a witch to live!"

"You're scum, Hopkins!" I spat. "You took my mother from me and now your curse is killing Marcus. Release him *now!*"

His defiant glare gave way to a look of confusion. He furrowed Marla's brow until her garish, white makeup cracked like a dried lake bed. "Twice this night you've accused the accuser, hag. I know nothing of your mother!"

"Release Marcus now and give me back my mother!" I screamed. Hot tears burned my eyes.

He fired me a menacing glare as I felt the energy from the dark spell that was killing Marcus begin to loosen its grip from around his neck.

"I said I know *nothing* of your mother's soul. If this be a trick, hag, remember the fate of your ally is bound to mine. If you destroy my essence, then you will destroy him!"

There was something about his tone that struck me as being genuine. Sure, I had no reason at all to believe the guy, but he'd just bound Marcus to his own fate and he was quite content to let my best friend die if I kept up the fight. I had every reason to call him a liar, but Hopkins truly seemed to believe that he had nothing to do with what happened to my mother.

"You attacked me at my school!" I growled. "You ripped my mother's soul from her body and now she's lying in a hospital bed waiting to die!"

Hopkins face was still awash with confusion, only this time there was a hint of frustration behind the burning embers that were Marla Lavik's eyes.

"I did no such thing, hag!" he raged. "I know nothing of your mother's soul. The only soul I am interested in this night is that of yours, witch!"

I didn't know what to do or say. He seemed to resent the insinuation that he'd somehow harmed my mother. Marcus was choking for air from a few feet away and I didn't have time to argue. If Hopkins had nothing to do with what happened to my mother then someone had been playing me. I was about to lash out at Hopkins again when I remembered who sent me to capture Matthew Hopkins' spiritual essence, and it was at that precise moment that I knew I'd been had.

Holly fucking Penske.

I threw a panicked glance at Marcus and saw that he wasn't moving. I had to end this now or he'd be as dead as my father. I couldn't destroy Hopkins' essence without harming Marcus, but nobody said I couldn't subdue the old spirit using non-magical means.

"Betty!" I shouted with ice cold fury. "I need your help now!"

Hopkins didn't see her coming. One hundred and thirty pounds of Great Dane leaped high into the air and dragged Marla Lavik's Goth-clad frame to the ground. I lowered my magic as Betty started mauling Marla's leather covered arms and I looked over at Marcus to see the death curse dissolve into ectoplasmic slime that drenched his entire body. I reached into my cargo pocket and pulled out my father's copper box and threw it on the ground beside Hopkins as he struggled in vain against Betty's immense strength. I scrawled a small chalk ring around the vessel and glowered at Hopkins. I bound my hatred of the Witchfinder General, my fear of losing my mom and Marcus into a final act of sheer will and lashed out with the rite of exorcism.

"Spirit!" I screamed with pent up rage. "Be released and take form within my ring."

Hopkins continued to struggle against Betty's crushing grip on his forearm, but to no avail. Marla's body went limp as a vaporous mass drifted out through her eyes and floated into the ring. I sent a small whisper of magic into the chalk circle and it snapped tight like a mousetrap.

"Speak thy miserable freaking name, spirit!" I growled. The supernatural mass twisted and churned inside the ring in a desperate attempt to resist my will. "Speak it!"

A disembodied voice called out from beyond. "Matthew Hopkins."

"Are you the same Matthew Hopkins known as the Witchfinder General of England? The same self-righteous loser that sent thousands to the gallows after accusing them and trying them for the crime of witchcraft?"

"I am," the disembodied voice rang out in a mournful, empty tone.

I exhaled heavily and bellowed in a clear and commanding voice, "Then it falls upon me to send you to your place of my choosing! Spirit of Matthew Hopkins, by my will I command you into yon vessel and blessed be!"

The tortured voice roared with every ounce of its four-hundred year-old hatred that it could muster. A wispy finger of magical light flew out of the vessel, trapping the vaporous mass and sucking it downward. It swirled and twisted against my magic and I could have sworn I caught a glimpse of Hopkins' bearded face before his entire spiritual form swirled into the vessel like water going down the drain. The lid flipped on its hinges and slammed shut with a tinny-sounding clang, and the locking bolt slid into place.

His ass was grass.

I raced over to Marcus and drew him into my arms, but he wasn't breathing. "Marcus, can you hear me?" I whispered in his ear. "Come back to me! Please come back!"

He still wasn't breathing so I opened his mouth and started puffing air into his lungs. His skin felt cold and clammy as I pressed two fingers against his neck in search of a pulse.

His heart wasn't beating. A crushing pain seized me. I let out a primal wail that echoed through the wrecked stadium as I pulled him against my chest.

"Don't go, Marcus," I sobbed, as I started rocking him gently. "Please don't do this. I read your letter, all those beautiful things you wrote. Just come back, okay? I need you. I can't do this without you, Marcus. Please, for the love of God come back to me!"

There was silence for a few more seconds and then I felt his heart slowly come back to life. He twitched a few times and then he stared up into my face and blinked weakly.

"Ow," he whispered.

And then something unexpected happened.

My thumping, panic-stricken heart *actually* skipped a beat.

"Marcus!" I cried, as I buried my face in his chest. "Oh, Marcus! Thank God you're alive!"

He coughed. "It's over?"

I nodded. "It's over. I've captured Hopkins and Marla is out like a light."

"Good," he said weakly. "Julie? Um, in my near death moment, I heard what you said about my letter. This might sound lame, but I left it out for you to see because I wanted you to know how I felt about you in case..."

I put two fingers on his lips. "Shhh. You don't have

to apologize to me, Marcus. It was a beautiful thing to do."

He nodded slowly and he gave me a relieved looking smile. "Hey, I was wondering if maybe this Friday night we could…"

"*Yes,*" I said quietly, as I leaned over and pressed my lips against his. He reached up and placed his hands against my cheeks and gently kissed me back with a tenderness and purity that sent waves of peace and contentment through my entire body.

"Ahem," Betty grumbled. "The girl is alive and we should take her home before the authorities get here and wonder why this stadium looks like ground zero of an earthquake."

I helped Marcus to his feet and he placed his hands on my waist. "Guess I can stop writing letters to you, huh?"

I gazed into his eyes and kissed him again. "Never stop writing about how you feel, Marcus. It was the most beautiful and touching thing anyone has ever done for me."

Marla slowly got up on her knees and glared at me.

"*You!*" she shrieked.

I snorted and stomped over to her. My Shadowcull's band tingled against my wrist and I raised my magic just in case she had another trick up her sleeve.

"You were supposed to be my *friend*, Marla," I snarled. "I don't know what kind of temporary insanity drove you to summon the spirit of Matthew

Hopkins!"

She started to giggle. She clutched her abdomen as her giggles turned into a fit of maniacal laughter.

"Oh yeah, she's lost it, Julie," Marcus said, as he walked up behind me. "Right off the deep end."

"It's not fair!" Marla raged. She scraped at the battered turf with her fingernails, throwing clumps of sod into the air. "You're a nothing – a *nobody!* Yet he loves you and you don't realize it until he nearly dies! He deserves better than you! He's always deserved better!"

Marcus knelt down in front of Marla and lifted her chin so that she could look into his eyes.

"In the real world, Marla, you don't get to decide who falls in love with you," he said coldly. "I've been friends with Julie for most of my life and she's *always* been there for me."

"She's a witch!" Marla screamed. "And you're probably enthralled by one of her spells!"

"I'm a *Shadowcull*," I growled. "And you have no business screwing around with magic. You're also damned lucky the covens didn't catch wind of what you did over the last few days."

Betty the dog nudged Marla's face with her slimy cold dog nose. "Be *silent*, girl!" she barked.

Marla slumped over and did a face plant in the grass as I reached over and scratched the crown of Betty's head.

"Nice one," I said with a thin smile on my face. "Is she going to be okay?"

"If her mind hasn't been torn to shreds by now, she should make a full recovery," Betty rumbled. "I've put her to sleep. She will be out for days. With any luck, she'll have learned her lesson."

"I hope you're right, Betty," I said grimly. "But my gut says we haven't heard the last from Marla. Come on, let's get her home."

## Chapter 27

We deposited Marla Lavik on her front step and quickly drove away. I sent Marcus home, too. He was probably up to his ears in trouble with his parents and I didn't want to add one minute more of stress to his, no doubt, permanently traumatized life. He protested, of course, but I was insistent: I had to face Holly Penske alone and because she was an immortal she could choose to do pretty much anything she pleased with either of us if we ticked her off. Marcus had nearly been killed saving my life and I absolutely refused to put him in danger ever again. He eventually agreed it was for the best and we made plans to go to a movie on Friday night, assuming he wasn't grounded until he finished college.

I also convinced Betty to stay home until she heard from me. This was less challenging than my debate with Marcus since Betty loathed Holly with every ounce of her being. I threw the vessel containing Matthew Hopkins' essence in my backpack and walked over to the

C-Train station. I didn't want to be in anyone's debt ever again. I'd captured the spirit of Matthew Hopkins so I'd kept up my end of the bargain.

As the train left the station, I considered her motives. Holly Penske, the one person in supernatural circles that nobody should ever be indebted to, set me up beautifully. If I wasn't so angry about it, I might have offered some measure of grudging admiration at her seemingly perfect logic. She knew I'd want to confront the poltergeist at Mrs Gilbert's. She staged the attack in my shed and the one at school, not to mention stealing my mom's soul. She put the video on YouTube and fabricated the persona of Hudibras, offering out clues like bread crumbs that would lead me to a confrontation with Matthew Hopkins.

When Marla summoned the old spirit in the washroom at school, Holly made her move. She took Mom's soul knowing full well that I'd do anything to get it back. It was a plan so convincing that Holly was certain I'd seek her counsel so that she could refer me to the one person who held the key to helping me take down what I thought was a practitioner named Hudibras: my father's ghost. It was only when I witnessed Hopkins' clear confusion after I accused him of stealing my mother's soul that I fully realized how easy it was for Holly to play me.

Being someone's pawn sucks ass.

The morning sun was sitting high in the sky and Bankers Hall cast long shadows over the streets of downtown Calgary. I had business to attend to, so I stomped up the marble corridor leading to the two rows of elevators and Star Corp Petroleum. My face was dirty, my hair a rat's nest, and my clothes were covered with grass stains, but it didn't matter. Holly had Mom's soul and her time was just about up. As I padded across the foyer and up to the snotty receptionist from you-know-where, it was everything I could do to stop myself from hexing her stupid computer. I was in a sour mood and the last thing I needed was another game of "let's screw over the teenager".

Imagine my surprise when she immediately stood up and smiled at me.

"Good morning, Ms Richardson," she said pleasantly. "Ms Penske was expecting you and wanted to tell you to head down to her office."

I cocked a wary eyebrow and grunted out something resembling a thank you, as I trudged down the gleaming granite corridor until I got to Holly's office door. I didn't need to knock, either. The door swung open and the smell of freshly brewed coffee filled my nostrils.

"Ms Richardson," she said in a super-friendly voice that made me want to punch her in the nose. "I see you're still alive so that must mean you have something I want very much in that bag of yours."

I tossed it onto her desk and took a seat in one of her huge leather office chairs.

I gave her a menacing glare. "My mother's soul; I want it back."

"Just as soon as we complete our transaction," she said, still smiling from ear to ear.

"It's done. Hopkins is inside my backpack in a copper box covered with sigils you'll probably recognize. I hope you realize I don't like being played for a fool."

Holly unzipped the backpack and pulled out the vessel. "There you are," she cooed as if she'd just found her lost cat. "It took me more than four hundred years to claim you, but your debt is paid and now you're mine."

I blinked hard. "Excuse me? What debt are you talking about?"

She pulled open a large bureau drawer and carefully deposited the box inside. "Why, Matthew Hopkins' debt to me, of course. He wanted to be famous so who do you think put the notion of becoming a Witchfinder in his head? They didn't exactly *elect* people in those days, young lady."

"So the poltergeist at Mrs Gilbert's house, the shed and the upturned lockers at my school – that was you, wasn't it? You're Hudibras."

"Indeed, I created the persona of Hudibras along with the video which I knew full well that you'd find," she said, her smile never wavering. "After I'd pulled Stearne into the mortal realm to attract your attention, I detected a series of summoning spells that were being used by an amateur practitioner. I probed the girl's mind to determine how I could manipulate her, and it didn't take much effort to learn that Marla Lavik was very much in love with your friend Marcus. It was the easiest thing in the world to make you her enemy because the girl knew that Marcus loves only you. I simply planted the seed in her mind that if she wanted Marcus for her own then she must destroy you. I convinced her that only the spirit of the Witchfinder General possessed enough hatred towards witches to make her magic powerful enough to kill. When the young lady was finally successful at summoning Hopkins in the washroom at your school, it seemed an opportune moment to manifest what *appeared* to be a poltergeist. I knew you would call your mother for assistance and that gave me the chance to acquire her soul. Only by harnessing the power of Endless Night could I ensure that you would eventually come to me."

I didn't give Holly a chance to say another word. Without thinking, I lunged across the desk with the sole aim of ripping her eyes out of their sockets, and Holly swept me aside with a wave of her index finger. I landed on the floor with a hard thud.

"Please, Julie, so immature," she clucked. "Surely you know that I am neutral on all things so kindly don't view me with scorn for simply carrying out my function."

"Your function?" I barked. "What gives you the right to meddle with people's lives, Holly? You were screwing me over the entire time! You kidnapped my mother's soul! My best friend nearly died!"

"Oh, don't be so morbid," she yawned. "I would have given it back. Your mother was in no danger."

"Her organs are shutting down and she had a seizure!" I barked again. "I knew nothing about your four hundred year-old arrangement with Matthew Hopkins and you made me become indebted to you so that you could possess his spirit! You used me!"

Her eyes narrowed and I thought for a moment she might lose her patience with me. "I did no such thing," she said in a cool voice. "If anything I've given you a great gift and you're no longer indebted to me – you gave me what I wanted and I gave you what you wanted."

"The only thing I wanted, Holly, was my mother to live. She would have never been at death's door if you hadn't orchestrated the events of the past two days. Why didn't you simply go after Matthew Hopkins yourself? If you have the power to pull the spirit of John Stearne back into the world of the living, clearly you can deal with a four hundred year-old ghost!"

Holly shrugged and said, "That, Shadowcull, is what mortals are for. But look at what you've gained! The events of the past two days have reunited you with your father. You've learned about your blood-line. Why, my actions have even drawn you closer, no doubt, to the boy you love, though you appear to have some competition in that regard. You see? No harm done."

I snorted. "Yeah. You just manipulated her jealousy."

She leaned back in her chair and tapped her index fingers together. "Oh, come now, Julie. It makes sense that in the flurry of activity you missed the fact that the young lady who summoned Hopkins did it for the sake of love. Really, I just don't understand why mortal females do these kinds of things to each other, but yes, I merely prodded her in a certain direction. I couldn't have taken advantage if the emotional motivation hadn't already been there."

"Seems like a hell of a way to eliminate the competition," I grumbled.

"In matters of the human heart you mortals have a terrible habit of stepping over the line that separates what you call good and evil," she continued. "This was *never* about your mother and I simply made good use of the girl's resentment toward you to achieve my goal. I'd keep an eye on that Marla girl – jealousy is a powerful ingredient that can fuel the blackest of magic. Well, that and of course something as small as one of your fingernail clippings or a strand of your hair."

I staggered for a moment as my mind flashed back to my encounter with Marla just before the attack at school. She'd taken a hair off my blouse; how could I have been so stupid not to have seen it coming? She used a part of me to not only summon Hopkins but to make her magic work. She'd planned the whole stinking thing and Holly just manipulated the circumstances to get her own desired result.

I clenched my jaw and pushed Marla's attempt on my life out of my mind. I defeated both Marla and

Hopkins at the Calgary Rugby Field, so if Marla had a brain in her head, she'd steer clear of me in the future.

"My mother," I said firmly. "How can I trust you after what you did? How will I know she's alive?"

Holly let out an impatient sigh and rolled her eyes. "Your cellular telephone still works, yes?"

I nodded and said nothing.

"In seven minutes, it will ring and you're going to hear your mother's voice. I recommend you exit Bankers Hall since we get frightfully bad reception in here for some reason or another."

I snatched my backpack from Holly's desk and reached inside. My cell phone still had half a charge, so I slipped it in my cargo pants and headed for the door of Holly's office.

"We're done, Holly," I growled. "Don't ever meddle in my life again."

Holly had a look of genuine disappointment on her face and she sighed heavily. "If that is your wish, Julie. Go now and be with your mother."

I was just about to step out the door when I spun around to face her.

"I thought you were leaving," she said.

"I will, but I have a question for you."

Her eyes narrowed again. "Be careful now, you don't wish to be indebted to me – you said so yourself."

I let out a dry chuckle. "This is a question that doesn't require payment, Holly. I just want to know why you chose me for this task."

She leaned over her desk and gave me a cold hard stare. "I chose you, mortal, because this was the first test. A test your father failed."

My cell phone rang, just as Holly said it would, and I sobbed in relief at the sound of Mom's voice. Unfortunately, the first words out of her mouth weren't exactly what I expected.

"You're grounded, kiddo," she said in a tired but angry voice.

"What for?" I squeaked, as if that was going to do any good.

"Because you didn't wait for me at school like I told you to. Because I'm in a bloody hospital bed due to your half-assed listening skills!"

"But Mom! You don't know what I've been through."

"Enough," she grumbled into the phone. "We'll discuss this when I get home."

Great. I save my Mom's life and I wind up getting grounded.

I started to chuckle and then the chuckle morphed into a fit of giggles. I laughed so hard that tears were pouring out of my eyes.

"I don't know what you think is so funny about all this, Julie," she said. "God, I sometimes wonder why I ever had children."

I choked back my giggles and sniffed a few times. "Mom, I love you, OK? Just remember that I love you so very much."

I heard her make a snorting sound, and then she said. "I love you too, sweetheart, but you're *still* grounded."

I missed my Friday night date with Marcus but it didn't really matter since he was grounded too. I boisterously lamented the loss of my newfound romantic life but it fell on deaf ears. Mom was still stewing about what happened and I wasn't going to make the mistake of increasing the punishment. We decided to take a rain check for about a month once our mutual punishments expired.

I still got to see him at school, though. The day after Mom got back from the hospital, Marcus had a run in with Mike Olsen who was bent on stuffing him in a trash can again.

"You are a total dweeb, Guffman," he taunted as he took a threatening step forward. "You ready for your daily dose of dweeb treatment?"

Marcus dropped his backpack at his side and let out a sigh. "I'm going to pose a question to you that will no doubt challenge your capacity for rational thought, Mike."

The giant defensive back folded his arms and his lips made a sly smile.

"Go for it, *loser*," he said in a deliberately slow drawl.

Marcus shrugged and took a confident step forward until he was inches from Mike's muscular chest. "Have you ever once in your life stared death in the face? I mean real honest-to-goodness death?"

"What?" the meathead replied with a smirk.

"Well, it changes you, Mike," Marcus' eyes narrowed menacingly. "It shows you the sheer insignificance of things like being popular at school or picking on people half your size and weight."

"Uh-huh," Mike replied sounding completely unimpressed.

"Want to know what else it does, Mike?" asked Marcus, his voice was cold and hard.

The lumbering football player blinked a few times as he looked Marcus in the eye. And a funny thing happened in that short moment of silence. I don't know whether it was Marcus finally standing up to the goon or whether he'd seen something in Marcus' eyes that actually frightened him, but Mike Olsen's cocky swagger simply vanished. He seemed to shrink a little as Marcus dug his finger into his chest.

"W-what?" he said nervously.

"It allows you to give other people a glimpse into hell itself, Mike," he said chillingly. "Mess with me again and I will *end* you. Got it?"

The colour drained from Mike Olsen's face completely and he bobbed his head up and down. "Got it," he whispered.

"Good," said Marcus as he dug his finger into Olsen's chest a little bit harder. "You have a nice day now, Mike."

I grabbed Marcus by the shoulder and then planted a tiny peck on his cheek as he turned on his heels. "That," I said in the best sultry voice I could muster, "was really stupid, really brave or really sexy."

Marcus threw his arm over my shoulder and pulled me in close. "How about all three?" he asked with a grin. "The new me is an amalgam of dashing, dumb and devoted. I've also had it up to here with the Mike Olsen's of the world."

I had to hand it to him. Two near-death experiences in as many days apparently gave my suitor a sharp new outlook on life and what I saw, I liked – even if his bony elbows were digging into my ribs as he gave me a full body hug. Well, that and the fact that we were going steady didn't hurt either.

"Your mom understands what happened, right?" he asked.

"Yep, but it didn't get me out of being grounded," I said flatly. "She's pretty freaked out about my having taken up the mantle of Shadowcull, too, but Dad smoothed things over. Of course, I think she's probably also ticked off about the new member of the family. She'd always wanted me to have a familiar, but I think her heart was set on a cat."

"Well Betty *is* a talking dog, Julie. Actually, she's a really big talking dog who can probably shoot laser beams out of her eyes if you asked her. Want to go get a Slurpee?"

I squeezed his hand as we trotted through the main

doors of Crescent Ridge High School and straight into the warm glow of the early autumn sun. Flecks of amber light glinted off my Shadowcull's band and I took a deep breath of the early autumn air. A dry gust of wind kicked up a small storm of fallen poplar leaves at our feet. I stopped for a moment and draped my arms around Marcus. He gave me a warm smile and I kissed him softly.

"I thought you'd never ask."

Julie's Grimoire
*September 30ᵗʰ*

*Somebody killed my father.*

This is the first entry in my new grimoire – I've decided to abandon Microsoft Word – yay me. I wanted to give it a cool name like "A Shadowcull's Diary" but Marcus pointed out that it's kind of a cheesy title. He's good, that way.

Mom is back to her old self though she's having a lot of trouble accepting the fact that I've taken my father's place as a Shadowcull. She confessed to me that she knew this day would come, she just wasn't expecting that I'd have to deal with all the dangers my father faced at this stage of my life. She'll be there to guide me, along with Betty, though the two of them rarely see eye-to-eye.

Everything points to Holly Penske, but I can't be certain as to what her motives are. She told me the attacks from the poltergeist at Mrs Gilbert's to the battle at the Calgary Rugby Stadium were a test. What I don't understand is how I could have passed a test that my father failed. Surely he could have easily captured the spirit of Matthew Hopkins; Dad possessed a lifetime of skill that I don't.

*Servo parvulus* – protect the child.

That explains why Mom has gone out of her way to keep me from danger, but from whom? Why? There's a ton of unanswered questions but my instincts tell me that if someone wanted me dead, it would have happened by now.

Was my father in Holly's debt?

From reading his grimoire, I've learned that he was on the trail of something far more dangerous than the spirit of the Witchfinder General. He was looking for a book that contained true names of players in the supernatural world because whoever found the book could bind anyone listed in its pages to their will. I wonder if Holly's true name is in that book. I wonder if that's why she put me to the test; to see if I had the power to replace my father as a Shadowcull. She might be an immortal sorceress, but everyone has something they fear more than anything. Is that what Holly fears? Falling under someone else's control?

All I know is that I've been swept into a world full of supernatural conspiracies that extend far beyond anything I could have imagined. Forces exist whose sole purpose is to prey on innocent people and I'm going to fight them. I'm going to protect those who can't protect themselves and if this is to become my life's work, then I can't think of anything I'd rather do more.

Somebody killed my father. I don't know who did it or why, but I'm going to find them.

I'm a girl.

I'm a witch.

I'm a Shadowcull.

Someone is going to pay.

# Acknowledgments

When I wrote the first draft for Poltergeeks more than two years ago, I had no idea that it would become "The Little Manuscript That Could". It started out as a cool idea which morphed into a really cool story with a great deal of potential, and I distinctly remember thinking "is this the book that will finally help me land an agent?" I knew I was onto something when I started querying and immediately received a lot of requests for partials. I got really REALLY excited when the same day I queried Jenny Savill at Andrew Nurnberg Associates, I received an email back saying:

> *I'm the agent responsible for nurturing our children's list here at ANA Ltd and I love your first three chapters! May I please see the whole ms?*
>
> *Is it out with any other agents?*

The last line told me that she was pretty damned

interested, and so began a wonderful working relationship. Both Jenny and her intrepid assistant Ella Kahn (who I would be *lost* without; utterly, hopelessly and tragically lost) saw the potential too. They put me through an intensive revisions process before I signed with ANA and even more intensive revisions after that. As a team, we scrubbed the living hell out of this story to the point of my printing it off and highlighting all of the romantic elements with a pink highlighter – that's where the story needed a ton of work.

And so I did as instructed – I revised and revised. I eventually finished those revisions in time for the Bologna Book Fair in 2011. Jenny and Ella were there cheering me on the entire time. In short, the reason you are reading this today is because of Jenny and Ella's great faith in me as a writer and in the potential for this book. I am both unbelievably lucky and incredibly grateful to have them in my corner.

Thank you to my editor Amanda Rutter who convinced me that:

a) Teenagers swear.

b) Marcus needs to stop taking crap from basically everyone.

c) Julie's Dad needed work.

d) Teenage daughters fight with their mothers. Like a lot.

Amanda has been a delight to work with and her enthusiasm for *Poltergeeks* knows no bounds. She's a genuine treasure and I look forward to working with her on the sequel.

I'd be a jerk if I didn't mention the Saskatchewan Romance Writers – particularly Hayley Lavik (whose surname I borrowed for Marla after Hayley gave me the okie-dokie) and Joanne Brothwell. Both gave me sound advice into the art of writing romance and any agents out there reading this should sign them both up. They're fantastic writers.

I'd like to thank authors Sara Grant, Nancy Holzner, Erin Kellison, Gary McMahon and Linda Poitevin for their lovely blurbs. To Paul Young for his incredibly breathtaking cover art, thank you, thank you, thank you! It's a hell of a thing to see your protagonist come to live in technicolor.

Thanks to Amilee Hagon and David Burkinshaw in Calgary for filming the promotional videos for the *Poltergeeks* book trailer – you guys rock.

And finally, thanks to Cheryl who is my ultimate sounding board for the entire writing process because she has an encyclopaedic knowledge of science fiction and fantasy – if it doesn't fly with Cheryl it will never get off the ground.

"It's like the best kind of video game: full of fun, mind-bendy ideas with high stakes, relentless action, and shocking twists!" – *E C Myers, author of* Fair Coin

"With whip-smart, instantly likable characters and a gothic small-town setting, Bond weaves a dark and gorgeous tapestry from America's oldest mystery." — *Scott Westerfeld*

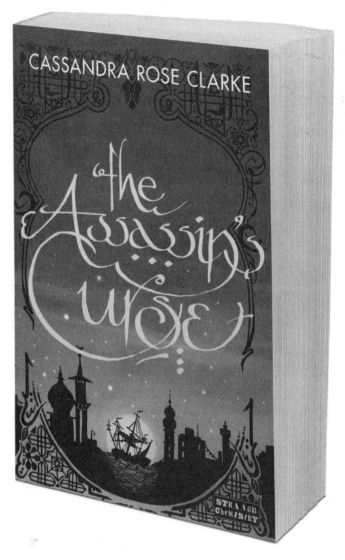

"Unique, heart-wrenching, full of mysteries and twists!"
— *Tamora Pierce*